DEV

Forbidden Love

in a Post Apocalyptic Dystopian Society

H J PERRY

Copyright © 2015 H J Perry

All rights reserved.

No part of this publication may be reproduced or transmitted by any means, electronic, mechanical, photocopying or otherwise without the permission of the publisher and author.

First edition.

Published by The Pandemic Press
Contact: helenjperry@outlook.com

Font for Cover & Titles is Credit Valley by Larabie Fonts Freeware Fonts http://www.typodermic.com

Print edition printed by createspace
ISBN-13:978-1505360615

Available in ebook format exclusive to Kindle from October 2015

Thank you.
All the people who made this
story what it is.
You know who you are.

Chapter One

The First Meeting

Contrary to the consensus, Mia concluded that desire for the opposite sex was natural. It was the very thing that had driven the successful reproduction and growth of the human species for millennia.

In a world that kept men locked away from women and at a time when acting on sexual desire was all on the down low she was a radical thinker. The extent of her practical, hands-on sexual experience was quite an achievement.

Over the past year, she transformed herself from virgin to deviant s-expert. She couldn't even remember the names of all the men she had met over the past year. She had simply gone along to the West Beach Men's Unit for the experience and enjoyed every minute of it. Well didn't exactly every minute, some of it hurt, was uncomfortable or didn't work well, in reality, in the way it had played out in her mind. She used the men like the disposable equipment in her in the laboratories. She was a scientist by profession and in her spare time experimented with men, learning from them, but she didn't consider it wrong. The men freely consented to take part, and they seemed to enjoy it.

Being confident with her sexuality didn't mean she would like to broadcast the details among her friends, family and work colleagues. Far from it, like all women who secretly sought out the company of men, Mia wanted complete discretion and for good reason. Other people aren't so broadminded, she could be shunned, loose her job or worse.

Mia couldn't stop thinking about Rayfe after their meeting. Perhaps because he was the first man she had ever met, therefore, the only man she had ever met at that time. Although there had been plenty of others since, there was something about her first man. Memories of him gave rise to feelings that couldn't be simply dismissed as naive infatuation. Thoughts and fantasies about him haunted her.

She had met many men since the first trip to West Beach, and no man had quite matched up to Rayfe. Either they were weren't as good looking or as charming or as gentlemanly as he was. She had made a couple of trips to West Beach every month and met a different man every time, amounting to in excess of twenty men. She had sex with most of them. She had also done her research, she was thorough as a scientist and decided to take the same approach to ensure that her encounters with men went the way she wanted. She read as many old books as she could find, this included digging deep in the university library archives for books about sex and sexuality written in the old era. Finally, when she was no longer an inexperienced virgin, she was ready to meet

Rayfe again as an equal. Ready to impress him.

Does it matter what he thinks when I am the paying client? But she knew it mattered to her.

Was she infatuated with a fantasy figure? Was he a character constructed in her imagination or was Rayfe, as the object of her desire, the man she remembered? What did she know about this man anyway, very little, nothing. He had only given her a massage some twelve months earlier on their first and only meeting, but there was something about him. Something she was going to put to the test today,

Mia was nervous about the consequences of that day's planned trip to West Beach, worried about it going wrong. He was at the center of her emotional as well as erotic fantasies and if, in reality, he failed to live up to those dreams tonight where would it leave her? Her secret life was exciting and the fantasies filled the empty hours between trips to West Beach. She had a successful career but outside of the science laboratory, life was lonely and lacked purpose.

Why was she meeting Rayfe tonight?

***

On the way to hut E12, Rayfe and Zander stopped off at the office to check their bookings. Just one client each, evening appointments, which was typical as most women worked in the daytime before making the journey from The Capital. Rayfe did didn't recognize the name, Mia, not one of his regulars, so he glanced at her client record. As a frequent visitor to West Beach she must be one of the wealthier clients.

When he looked down the long list of names to see when this client started to visit the unit he was surprised to see his own name as the very first man she had ever seen, over a year ago, and now she was booking him for a second time. He double-checked the list again to see if his first impression was correct, it was, she had never seen a man twice until today. Why today? Why him? If anything, he would have expected a repeat appointment soon after her first, not after sampling twenty or so other men. Even after reading his own report of the session, he couldn't remember anything about it at all, hardly surprising after more than twelve months had passed, along with hundreds of one-night stands with other women.

At twenty-nine she was the same age as him, always a good thing as he was more attracted to women around his own age and that made his job a little bit easier. It was so much better to fuck a woman if you fancied her. Mia was a regular visitor to the gentlemen of West Beach, her record revealed, she had seen a different man every two or three weeks, with no discernible pattern to her choice of partners. She seemed to like variety; they had been all ages and ethnic types. Men usually made confidential notes about what happened in a session, but only the man who wrote them could read them. Rayfe often wondered, what was the point of the confidentiality? They all knew what went on, and they all did much the same things. It might just be handy if the card told him the sort of things this woman particularly liked, but there was no helpful information at all.

At least today's session required no preparation because she hadn't requested anything specific.

Sometimes they asked for certain rooms, clothes or scenarios. Today he simply had to turn up, turn on the charisma when needed and pretend he remembered her. No problem, he had his strategy. Rayfe relied on charm and flattery, make them feel special, don't rush to get their pants off. A strategy that seemed to work as he had many regular clients.

With no planning to do, the day was his own, which was just as well, as he was moving home. Hundreds of residents at the West Beach Unit for Adult Men were moving out of overcrowded dormitories in the main building into slightly less cramped rooms. The rooms were only for sleeping but with up to ten grown men in a room, everyone welcomed the prospect of more space, less smelly socks and fewer voices in the chorus of snores. Almost a hundred small sleeping units had been erected in the grounds, in an area that used to be called The village, as it already comprised a few outbuildings including dwellings. Due to the current expansion, The Village was increasingly looking like a town.

The new units appeared to be little more than wooden shacks, giving the appearance of a medieval shantytown. The outer wooden cladding hid modern insulating materials, which meant the accommodation was perfectly suitable for sleeping in the modern era, regardless of what the coastal weather could throw at them. The solar panels on every roof were the only external sign that these might be modern dwellings rather than nineteenth-century garden potting sheds.

"So, you're going to be head of the room because you've been here almost twenty years," Rayfe said to Zander as they walked through the narrow passageways looking for their door. Background music from a steel band performing at the recreation arena rang out across the village creating a carnival atmosphere.

"Not quite, I'm not that old," Zander interrupted.

Rayfe knew Zander was thirty-five. Men moved to West Beach when they were nineteen, so it was hardly advanced maths. "Whereas with only ten years under my belt I might be qualified to be your deputy," he continued.

Rayfe and Zander had been roommates for several years, and their new destination kept them together.

"Will we need a third in command? I guess we won't know until we find out what the others guys are like. Here it is, E12, our new cottage."

They walked straight in; doors at West Beach were usually left unlocked if they had a lock at all. There was a table in the center of the room with six chairs tucked underneath. The room was cold and bare but luxuriously spacious compared to what they were used to. Squeezed between the three sets of bunk beds there were cupboards with space for hanging clothes, shelves and drawers. A sink hung on the wall in the corner at the back of the room.

"Great result," said Rayfe, looking at the paper on the table. "12E is a room for six but with only four names on the list. Jay is in this room with us, we know Jay, and Paul, a new guy. I don't know him."

"It seems fair to me," replied Zander. "Four in this room. As big as we are, we need the space." By any measure, Rayfe was tall and broad except when compared to Zander. The wild looking giant of Native American heritage, with long black hair, dark eyes and inked arms the girth of tree trunks.

"I'm happy with that, just hope he doesn't talk in his sleep." Of the many things sociable, outgoing Jay was known for, excessive talking was one of them.

"I didn't think to check that out; I just assumed he must eventually wear himself out." Zander pulled out one of the chairs and sat down.

"Hold on, you didn't need to look at that list did you?" Rayfe said staring up at Zander accusingly.

Zander gestured mock surprise. "What do you mean?"

"You knew all along but didn't tell me who's in our room."

"Of course I knew," Zander leaned back and placed his hands behind his head. "I talked about it with Walsh; I like to think I had some input planning this group. I have a message from her actually, but that can wait until the others get here."

"If you had anything to do with there being just four of us in a six-man room, then good work." They may be friends and roommates but Rayfe had no right to expect Zander to tell him everything. He couldn't be mad with him when the result worked well for them.

***

A little over a year ago he was the first man she had ever met. She had been apprehensive about that meeting. One part of her wanted to rip his clothes off, another part wanted to do nothing and hoped he would tear her's off and behave like the impulsive animal that men were rumored to be. Another part of her felt that the adventure was a bad idea, and she should just run away to safety. Torn by her feelings she was relieved when he turned out to be nothing like the monster of her worst fears. He took control of the situation, but he was a gentleman and put her at her ease. Since that time, he had been the object of her fantasies.

She clearly remembered his olive complexion, bronzed skin even though it was nearing the end of months of a cold dark winter. A genetic heritage originating from more southerly latitudes when world travel was once possible and the population was counted in billions. Before the pandemic.

The ruggedly handsome man with his thick black hair was tall enough and strong enough to be frightening, but nothing about him was; he was everything she had hoped for in a man.

That first time he had suggested they massaged each other and gave her the choice of whether she wanted to go first or second. As a team leader and expert in her field in her normal daily life, she was ill prepared for feeling ignorant and out of control.

"I don't know anything about massage," she said.

"What about if I massage you, you can see what it feels like, and then you can have a go on me if you want to."

Not trusting her voice, she nodded.

"We'll start with hands," he said pulling up two straight-backed chairs. They sat close together, facing each other. Her knees were together his long legs either side of hers, enveloping her; she felt small and vulnerable.

Mia held out her hands, not knowing what to

expect. Rayfe took them and they looked so delicate in his; he placed one on his own leg, he gave his full focus to the other, massaging one tiny part of her anatomy.

I actually have a hand on a man's leg, she thought, barely believing it was real, both of her hands felt as if they were on fire.

From childhood, girls learned that men are loud, aggressive and violent but this man was gentle, his voice was soft, and his hands were nurturing. He showed every sign of caring about her, even though they had only just met.

Holding hands like that was excruciatingly intimate, something Mia had never before experienced. It was as if their very souls were mingling through this gentle touching of skin.

"Do you want to have a go?" She was unprepared for how helplessly inexperienced and naive she felt.

Each of his hands was so much bigger than hers, the fingers longer and thicker, with neatly manicured nails that were a little longer than she would have expected. She thought she could detect the strength in the tiny muscles and noted the texture of the skin, different to that of her own, thicker and tougher, with short black wiry hairs on his fingers. The pads of the fingertips were hard, covered in a layer of tough skin. Aware of his eyes on her face she couldn't lift her own from studying his hands.

"Let me do your shoulders next, it will help you relax," he said.

As she sat in the chair, he massaged her shoulders, her head, her arms, her back through her clothing, an Indian Head Massage he called it. It felt amazing, not sexual, intimate, incredibly relaxing and perhaps sensual. Her nerves calmed, and she began to feel at ease enjoying the close contact.

When she felt him move close to the back of her head and his breath next to her ear she prepared herself for a kiss that didn't come and she suppressed a shiver of anticipation.

"Would you like to do the same to me?" His deep voice reverberated through her.

"Yes."

Yes, I want to touch you, that's why I'm here. I don't know what I'm doing, but I'm here now.

She continued sitting, trying to refocus and bring herself back down from the cloud she felt she had floated up to while enjoying his touch. He walked around to stand in front of her.

"Then I'll take my shirt off, it will make it easier for you."

She noticed he had already undone several of his buttons, and he was working on the rest.

His trousers hung low and loose, a line of dark hair ran like an arrow from his navel disappearing into the top of the fabric pointing to, who knew what. Mia took some deep breaths as she felt herself flush. He stood, his bare chest exposed, shirt discarded within seconds. This must be deliberate, this not-so-innocent strip show in front of her. She couldn't have picked a better man for this. Tall, broad and muscular with a hairy chest, he was as masculine as she had imagined but far more considerate. She loved him for giving her what she wanted, the chance to see and ogle a hairy chest and now to touch his body. He made it all seem so innocuous and natural instead of a deeply shameful activity. Here he was standing half-naked before her and making it look like sex was not on their minds.

"It would be easier if you stand and I sit," he prompted.

Of course, it would. Without giving her a moment to feel stupid he picked up something and handed it to her.

"If you put this powder on your hands it will help them move over my skin easily. Use it liberally. Don't worry about getting it everywhere, like on our clothes, because it just brushes off."

He sat down in the chair that she vacated.

She took a deep breath. This was it. For the very first time she was going to touch the body of a man, and it was going to be good.

With no experience of touching bare skin other than her own, let alone massage, Mia followed the instructions and coated her hands in the fine white dust.

"Is this right?" Her voice squeaked, strangled by nerves. She held out her white hands for approval.

"Yes plenty and you'll know if you need more."

She placed her powder-coated hands on his shoulders, they felt broad and solid compared to her own. Her hands moved away from his neck across his shoulders and down his arms. Feeling solid muscle, with strength greater than any woman's, was both scary and exciting. Scary because of what masculinity represented, scary because like all women she had been taught to be frightened of men. Exciting, simply because it was exciting. She couldn't help how she responded to this attractive man, he was the antithesis of femininity, and she found it intoxicating.

Savoring every moment, touching those arms, feeling her hands on his broad back, she moved closer to him and let her hands sweep up over his shoulders and down on to his chest, across the rug of fine soft hair. In effect, she had her arms around him and was so close she could kiss him. Embarrassment suddenly overwhelmed her, and she began to pull away, but his hands took hold of hers.

"Before you leave will you kiss me?" he whispered, holding her there, close to him. The request astounded her. Will you kiss me? He had asked her, putting her in charge; he didn't ask if he could kiss her.

She wanted to. She wanted to do much more as well, but this was all new and not how she wanted it to be. She was uncomfortable with her role as the timid virgin.

"Thank you," she said politely, "I have to go."

She pulled her hands away and before he had the opportunity to respond she ran out of the room, hands and clothes still covered in powder.

What a fool she had been to rush out after she had paid good money to do what she wanted with that man. She knew why she left. Everything was so overwhelming. It was her first time. She had never kissed anyone, except in a sisterly way, never touched a man, and never even met a man before. She certainly felt full of desire but also held back by a lifetime of education and fear. She was attracted to Rayfe, but her lack of experience both embarrassed and paralyzed her.

What must Rayfe have thought of her? He probably laughed at her or didn't give her a second thought.

More than a year had passed since that humiliating experience, so will he still remember her, all this time later? Perhaps that incident is long forgotten, after all, it must have been no big deal for him. Women pay to spend time with him every day, and they probably have a far sexier time. Yes, that's it, if he thought anything, he probably thought she was silly. Well, he would be left with a very different impression after their session tonight.

&&&

"Men are different to women in many ways, not just those you can see.

For lengthy periods of time they can appear civilized in their behavior, just like women.

But they are liable to impulsive actions including aggression and violence.

They are extremely competitive and often uncooperative.

The dominance of society by males may explain why history can be summarized as a list of conflicts, wars and inhumanity before the current era of Matriarchy."

*extract from Her-Story,
text book for school girls
published when Mia's grandmother was a child.*

Chapter Two

Moving

"I've an important welcome message from Walsh." Zander stood up from the table as if to make an important speech, even though there were only three people in this audience.

Rayfe and Paul glanced up from their bottoms bunks, where they were lounging. Jay turned from his unpacking to give his full attention.

"She wanted me to tell all of you that she's put us together not just because she thinks we'll get on well. She thinks it will be good for us. We should all be among the top earners here so we should be together encouraging each other and helping each other. Working together as a team."

"So, you're saying Walsh wants me to let you all in on my secret ways with the ladies," said Rayfe. "How to charm them and keep them coming back for more?"

"Yes please," Jay turned away from the cupboards looking towards Rayfe, leaving his sorting-out half done.

"Flatter them, make them think they're extra special and whatever you say to them, try to mean it." Rayfe stretched out on the bunk feeling a little smug and content. A new room with good companions, nothing could be better. "I can't tell you the exact words I use because that's top secret, and it wouldn't do for you to deliver the same speech to a woman who has heard it all before, from me."

With Zander's words on his mind about them being a team of top earners, it struck Rayfe just how good-looking the two young men appeared, in a youthful and pretty way. Both were slim, with captivating blue eyes. Tall too, probably around six feet or perhaps a little over. They could easily have been brothers. They were a stark contrast to the rugged and wild looks of Zander and himself.

"Why is Walsh sending this message?" asked Paul. At nineteen he was a new comer to West Beach and had just finished his induction training period.

"She was your individual teacher through your induction. We four were all taught by her. She continues to have a role as a counselor, that is as a supporter or adviser if you like. Even though I might only see her once a year or so," Zander explained. "She has the same responsibility for a few hundred of the men here. All of the counselors are in competition, so Walsh wants to help the men under her wing be more successful than any of the others."

"More clients here helps fund all the Men's Units." Paul said, as if thinking aloud about the unit in which he'd grown up and left behind only a few months earlier. His head fell back and his eyes rolled as if to study something on the ceiling.

"You know that more credits mean more luxury

and making it onto the WB leader board." At twenty three, blonde-haired Jay had been at West Beach for four years. He addressed his comment towards Paul and turned back towards his unpacking.

Although Jay was right, Rayfe thought his comments were far from hitting the correct mark.

"The best way we can help the families we grew up with is by doing well here so there are more supplies to send back. I lived at Eb's Farm before coming here. I didn't realize how impoverished we were there or that the supplies that did come in were funded by the men working here." Rayfe hoped Paul would find some comfort in this fact, rather than hopelessly pine for a home he would eventually forget.

"Each day I wake up pleased to be here and instead of back there," Jay added.

"Success, measured in terms of credits also enables you to choose what job you do," Zander explained.

"Yeah. What really appeals to me is choosing the community work, which you can if you are on the leader board," Jay chipped in.

Rayfe was pleased they didn't dwell on thoughts of the other Men's Units, dreary places that were rarely spoken of. "Today I'm on cleaning, this whole month I'm on cleaning, emptying bins, scrubbing showers; I don't know what is worse."

"I'm cleaning too, this month, I prefer doing the dusting and polishing if I get the chance on cleaning duty. No-one volunteers for cleaning toilets and showers," Jay said.

"Me too, I'm cleaning too." Paul got off his bed and pulled a chair out to sit at the table.

"Sorry kid, new boys usually get the worst

jobs," Rayfe replied.

"And we're all on cleaning then but at least it is reduced hours on community work today due to the big move," said Zander pulling out a chair too.

"And that's why those drums are sounding out this morning, I suppose," Jay commented. "They're deafening when you're up near them and we've all got to walk past them to get out of the main building. I looked for you there Zander; I thought you might be among them, thumping away."

"I don't play the steel drums," Zander stated with a far away look on his face.

"I thought you banged everything, mind the pun," Jay tapped on the nearest bed frame to punctuate his joke.

"Women yes, but not quite everything. All drums aren't the same." Zander was known across the unit, not just for his looks and his politics but for his percussive talents. He was a drummer but most often seen with a durable African djembe.

"I can't blame you for the racket then."

"It isn't a racket; I like it." Paul interjected.

"Thank you." Zander lifted a hand palm outstretched to indicate an ally while Jay raised his eyebrows.

"He might not be banging the drum in person but you can thank Zander for the musical accompaniment to moving day," said Rayfe, moving into a sitting up position on his bed.

"How come?" Paul asked.

"Mr Percussion here had the good idea that there should be some get-up-and-go music to help us get up and go." Rayfe sounded as if he disapproved but, in fact, he loved music and this was just the way he interacted with his oldest and closest pal at West

Beach.

"Well it's worked, there's a great party atmosphere out there."

"Thank you, Paul, that's what I said when I suggested the steel band, plus, none of the men performing in the band is actually involved in the room change. They're sleeping in the same bed tonight."

"In which room would that be?" Rayfe asked.

"What?"

"Where is the massive bed? The one big enough for all the drummers sleeping in the same bed tonight?"

Smiles slowly appeared on the faces of all in the room as what Rayfe had said was dawning on them.

"Do you play anything Paul?" asked Zander.

Paul's expression was blank.

"He means music. I play the guitar; Zee's a drummer," Rayfe explained.

"No, I don't play anything, except sport, of course."

"Zee could set you up on percussion if we have any room jam sessions."

"Room jam would be cool," Jay nodded his agreement. Turning to the new man and nodding towards Rayfe he explained, "We are lucky to be sharing a room with the Paco de Lucia of our age."

"Pacu du who?"

"Don't worry about it Paul, Jay's just qualified to be the leader of my fan club." Rayfe was flattered to be associated with one of the great musicians of the old era. He added, "You'll learn now you're living with musicians."

The three musicians in the room grinned.

Rayfe hadn't realized until this point what three

of them had in common. They were among the most proficient musicians at West Beach, always beings asked to perform. As they all played different styles of music they didn't practice together, so he hadn't instantly identified that connection between them. A coincidence perhaps, or thanks to Zander's influence upon Walsh.

"Anyone booked today?" Rayfe changed the conversation.

Paul and Jay shook their heads, and everyone turned to Rayfe, "Yes. Tonight, early evening. I don't know anything about her. What about you, Zee?"

"I'm booked too, a regular in the afternoon. You never know, something may turn up for you guys at the last minute. Sometimes women call for a last minute, spur of the moment appointment, so it is always worth being ready to go."

"I hope so," Jay said. "I can't be going for days without, days like yesterday when all the clients canceled. There are things a young man has got to do."

"I hope you aren't on a one man mission to soil the showers?"

"I'm trying to avoid it," Jay grinned. "Needs must. But stuck down here in the new village with just one big communal shower block, if ever there was an incentive to get full satisfaction when on the job." Everyone laughed as Jay thrust his pelvis in time with his story. "I don't want to have to walk all the way to the main building and up the stairs only to find there's a queue for those individual showers when I need a private hand shake."

When the men stopped laughing Jay resumed his unpacking.

Rayfe thought about his next move.

"You can get clients almost every day," said Zander. "Ray and I used to room-share before this, and we are in the habit of getting to the office as early as possible in the mornings. Every day, sessions become available for any man to take so if you are always there, checking in at the office, you can get those before the others get a chance."

"That's true," Rayfe agreed. "Also working as a team can mean getting work for each other. Such as when people are looking to make up numbers for a group session or a client asks for a recommendation, we should think about each other and not just ourselves."

"Yes, Ray's right. We should be doing that for each other." Jay agreed.

"As we are all on cleaning, shall we go up to work together then, as soon as we are all unpacked? I'd like to get it over with, especially as I am booked tonight," said Rayfe.

"Together, for a room 12E pushing brooms bonding experience sounds lovely." Jay quipped.

&&&

"Only those who have proven abilities above and beyond the average are selected for a Military posting at West Beach Unit for Men

It is unlike any other Men's facility.

As the only center for fertility, the men at West Beach are healthy and have high levels of testosterone.

West Beach is unique in that it is the only unit

DEVIANT

where ALL of the men are free of inhibitors.

As you are aware, at other units all of the adult males over the age of twenty are carefully controlled by a cocktail of chemicals, along with most of the teenagers,

Consequently, all guards must be vigilant at all times and all men monitored closely.

As at all Unit's, the men must be treated with respect, as valued clients.

Above all, it is vital that this unit is protected from terrorists.

Security at West Beach is of the highest order, it is a matter of world security."

Extract from the TOP SECRET introductory letter sent to military personnel prior to a posting at West Beach

Chapter Three

Paid

Mia was sitting in one of the private rooms waiting for her "date" to arrive. She was very early, which gave her time to prepare. It was one of the basic rooms, so it had a bed with side tables. Condoms, lube and tissues were in the top drawer alongside a selection of massage oils and powder. Mia didn't need to look; she knew this arrangement was standard everywhere at West Beach. The essentials were readily at hand without actually being on display. In addition to a large comfortable bed, obviously an essential, there were a couple of chairs and a door through to an ensuite shower room.

Music in the room through the fitted speakers was optional, a dial controlled the volume all the way down to off; a switch toggled between the two music sources. Prerecorded music came from channel one, whatever was playing on the loop for the day. Alternatively an eclectic mix of live music was intermittently available on channel two along with coughs, mistakes and the sound of tuning up, some of it was superb. Mia chose the live music, something classical, and turned the volume to a quiet setting.

She stood up as he walked in. He strode purposefully towards her but she noticed he hesitated as his eyes moved up and down her body taking in the full picture in just the way she had hoped he would. He was taken aback by her appearance. He wasn't the only one in the room who looked alluring, and she knew it. Through her months of learning and preparation, she had discovered the importance of visual impact, something she wouldn't have thought about a year ago. She had dressed in a black pinafore dress; it was shorter than anything she would normally wear but not improbably short. A bright red blouse shouted out from under the sexy piceous dress. She was also wearing black, high-heeled, for-the-bedroom-only shoes and black stockings.

He looked every bit as gorgeous as she remembered. Tall, dark and handsome, rugged and manly in contrast to some of the men she had met, men who might more aptly be described as pretty or even beautiful. He was wearing low-slung denim jeans and a loose, black, knitted sweater, at least it would have been loose on her but fitted his broad, muscular shoulders snugly. Rayfe was casual but very sexy.

He looked so pleased to see her, his eyes full of recognition. He reached her in just a few strides and took her hands in his.

"I'm so pleased you've come back," he said looking her straight in the eyes. "I kept wondering what I could have done differently, and now I'm so pleased to get a second chance with you."

"Do you say that to every woman on her second

visit?"

"No. I only say what I feel. I can't help it. When I met you, it was like nothing else I've experienced. When I look into your eyes, I see an amazing woman. A woman I want to get to know."

Mia became aware of her body pressed up against his, a heat passing between them. Had he moved closer? No, she realized she was drawn to him. She was unable to keep away, like iron to a magnet.

"There was something between us and I think you felt it too, that first time. Is that why you left so suddenly?"

So he did remember. His face had moved down closer to hers, his lips were so close, within kissing distance.

"Yes," Mia whispered. She stood up on tiptoes to kiss him. She took the initiative, and she pushed her lips against his.

He let go of her hands and slipped his arms around her waist, she reciprocated. Locked in an embrace their lips pressed together, the tips of their tongues touched, curled, burrowed in to explore each other's mouths.

Mia moved her hands under his jumper and found his bare skin, he flinched a little.

"I'm sorry," she said but without drawing away.

"Don't be," he replied, his lips brushing against hers. "You can feel the chemistry between us."

Was he making a statement or asking a question, being observant or giving her subliminal messages? She couldn't be sure.

She was losing her self-control too quickly, he was charming, sexy and so very disarming. She needed to assert herself and demonstrate that she was no longer the awe-struck virgin he might remember, she was flattered that he liked her but wanted to make him as hot as he made her. Her index fingers tucked inside the top of his trousers and slowly move around to the front. He must have felt the movement across his hips, it could have tickled but he showed no acknowledgment. When she reached his fly a flick with her thumb undid the top button, a few similar movements and his trousers were completely undone. Mia could see the surprise in his face as she pulled her lips away and sunk to her knees.

Yes, she thought, you weren't expecting this.

There was no hiding the surprise on his face but the size of his swollen cock, as she loosened it from his jeans, confirmed her every instinct. This was something he liked. With one hand holding the shaft, she let her other hand cradle his balls as her tongue gently licked the tip of his head. It tasted clean. These men were always so clean, but he was not going to stay that way.

She pushed the trousers below his knees and continued to lick slowly in ever increasing circles around the head of his cock and then down the length, not stopping. She licked and sucked his balls while moving her hand very lightly along inches. She did it so softly that she could imagine him begging for more though she was also sure he wouldn't ask for anything, remaining completely professional at all times. She licked the sides of his dick again and then took it in her mouth, slowly she sucked him, taking in as much as she could, savoring the taste of the surfacing salty precum.

Mia looked up and was pleased to see Rayfe had his eyes shut and his mouth open, he looked lost in the moment with a hand out on the wall to steady himself. He wasn't looking at her, deliberately perhaps. Perfect, she thought as she continued teasing him with her mouth while her fingers explored the area. Stroking his thighs, his balls, passing through his legs, her fingernails scratching his buttocks and gently teasing his crack. He was making slight groans, and she could tell he was doing all he could to hold back from thrusting. He must be on the edge, and I brought him here, Mia thought to herself, thrilled.

She pulled her mouth from his cock and spoke clearly, "If you need to come, you go ahead."

And she sucked it in again. This time she felt it pulsate, and sure enough a moment later his salty spunk filled her mouth. She didn't take her eyes off his face as her mouth worked, hungrily swallowing until there was no more, and she had completely cleaned him with her tongue.

His eyes were open now, watching her with a dreamy, pleased-with-himself dazed look on his face.

She stood up, and he did nothing but look at her as if he were in a trance.

"I think we might be more comfortable on the bed," she said. "Step out of these trousers, take off your top and lie down."

He smiled at her and said dreamily, "You're beautiful."

"On the bed," she repeated, and he obeyed.

Without removing any of her own clothes, Mia followed him and when he was lying down she straddled his stomach. Only now, as he felt the bare flesh at the top of her legs would he realize she was wearing stockings. She hoped he would appreciate them, surely all men are turned on by them. The tops of the stockings, the suspenders and the garter belt all served to frame the parts that are rarely seen, beautifully.

"I did enjoy that," she said, with a naughty grin that she hoped conveyed much more. "Now I think it's my turn, are you ready?"

"I'm ready to do anything for you." As always his words sounded sincere but Mia sensed they revealed nothing, he may well say the same thing to every woman.

She moved up the bed and stopped far enough from his face for him to get a good view, to take in the fact that she had been wearing no panties the whole time, and now she was touching her pussy.

"Do you think you can do something with this for me?"

"Bring it here," he replied. Right answer.

Nice though it was to sit across his face Mia was so wet and turned on that it was going to take a lot more than one man's tongue to satisfy her. Before she could decide on the next course of action Rayfe used his initiative, he placed one hand on her ass with the other he fingered her pussy while all the time licking and sucking her clit. As she ground her hips into his face, he increased the tempo, thrusting his fingers inside her at a perfect pace and soon she was thrashing and screaming with pleasure as her orgasm seized her.

***

Like a gush of warm water from a shower, her juices drenched his already wet face. Rayfe had been here before, of course. Licking a woman to beyond orgasm was an occupational pastime, an everyday occurrence though it didn't typically happen after his cock had been sucked quite like that. Hell, his cock was rarely sucked like that.

Rayfe had felt guilty, everything he had learned and done over ten years working at West Beach providing sexual services to women, proved the rule that you don't come until the lady is satisfied. It didn't always work out that way, of course. Never in his decade as a professional provider of pleasure and with countless women, hundreds of different women, in thousands of sessions, never had he allowed himself an orgasm when he hadn't even touched the woman. In fact, he flattered himself to think he couldn't remember coming before any woman had come at least once, even if she weren't finished.

He was shocked and upset by his lack of self-control; confused by what had just happened. It was something he wasn't supposed to do, though it felt leg-wobblingly good, and she had urged him on. The look on her face after he came reassured him that was what she wanted.

Mia turned the tables on him and made him feel like the object of desire, but it wasn't that simple. Women liked Rayfe because he was young and good-looking, and so he was their object of desire. He played on that, seducing them. He'd use his notes as a guide, for the right things to say and do. As he had with Mia tonight, he couldn't remember anything about their previous meeting, but it happened, and he had seen his notes.

The way this particular lady behaved, however, was different. It was as if she wanted to turn him on and make him come. When he did, and she swallowed every last drop the look on her face was arousal mixed with triumph. Women didn't usually pay much attention to getting a man off but Mia wanted to, and Rayfe saw that in her. Clients don't usually suck dick and eat cum like that, he noted.

Rayfe became aware of his arousal, of his hard cock moving for attention again. Such a fast recovery no doubt provoked by such a sexy situation, such a sexy, amazing woman. He lifted her off him, and she seemed happy to collapse on the bed beside him, but he wasn't going to let her think that was all he could do. He had some face-saving showing off to do to make up for his premature lack of control. He got off the bed in a flash. He was about to get a condom when he had another thought. She was watching him.

"You like my cock, don't you?" He stood next to her stroking it, presenting it hard and ready for more action. He already knew she liked it; the rhetorical question was just to focus her attention.

She licked her lips slowly, and Rayfe saw the suggestive look on her face.

This woman is such a turn on; he thought, and his cock got even harder.

"You look fantastic, so sexy; I can't remember the last time I saw stockings," he said, back on to familiar ground giving out the compliments. Women love being flattered, and it was easy when he meant every word.

"It looks like you want something" she replied.

It's not about what I want, it is all about you and what you want.

"I want to fuck you. I want you on your knees here at the end of this bed, so I can lift up that short skirt of yours." He gave an honest answer.

She grinned and quickly moved to oblige. Rayfe put on a condom. He stood for a moment contemplating the view in front of him. He put both his hands on her buttocks and then moved one hand down between her legs to her pussy, it was dripping. He moved his hand forward between her legs and felt her hard clit. He didn't focus on her clit, but continued past, touching her stomach and reaching under her all the way to her breasts, knowing that his arm would be stimulating her as it pushed between her thighs brushing against her sensitive areas. He pulled his hand back. Again, the languid movement over her pussy, he could sense her arousal; she moaned, moving slightly, arching her back and pushing against him.

He positioned himself and entered. She moaned, and he realized he did too. This was his daily work, but the build-up was rarely like this. When had he seen a woman dressed like this? Not often. Not just for him alone in private. There was something very sexy about fucking a woman still in her clothes when he was naked. What is she doing? He felt her hands feeling the base of his cock as it drove in and out of her; the fingers weren't stopping there though. She reached down to his balls and squeezed them gently.

Why are you doing this? I'm supposed to turn you on, not the other way round, I'm the one working here so what are you doing?

"I love the feeling of you fucking me," she said, "and seeing you so turned on." She answered his question but how did she read his mind? "I want to feel you fucking me hard."

What could he do, only as he was told? He rammed into her until she came. It was all he could do to hold back, but he did. He had to because he couldn't lose control again so quickly, what would she think of him. Did it matter? She wouldn't book him again anyway, she liked variety, remember. That made it even more vital to make this one and only session last.

She collapsed on the bed, energy all spent, but still with just enough reticence to roll over and look at him.

"What do you like? Like for yourself?" she asked. How could she maintain such a cool exterior after the earth shattering orgasm she just appeared to enjoy?

Had a client ever asked him that before? The trite answer, *pleasing you,* seemed completely wrong now. *I don't know*, but that seems pathetic. *Think. Think. What has she done to me? Honesty, the best method is to mean what you say.*

"I've never had sex like this before. How you're dressed, how you've sucked me, it's blowing my mind."

"I can give you some more of that, come and lie down."

He didn't think about it but lay down on the bed. She removed the condom and proceeded to suck his cock, hard, not as the restrained teasing of earlier. He tried to touch her, but she pushed his hand away.

"No, this is for you."

Rayfe lay back and did something he didn't normally do with women; he just lay there. Not thinking, not plotting his next move. He focused on what he was feeling. He felt almost giddy as if he were floating out of control. It was a feeling that lasted for ages; it could have been minutes or hours. The serene sensation gave way to more powerful desires, a need to thrust, a need. His whole body experienced the orgasm as it swept through him, he came, selfishly pushing his cock into her eager mouth until he needed to thrust no more, he wearily collapsed back into the comfortable soft sheets.

***

Mia lay next to Rayfe and watched him sleeping. For a moment she was concerned, she had never seen a man sleep before, and many of her previous visits had involved a lot of physical activity for a much longer period. As she watched him, she realized that he slept because he was relaxed, totally relaxed in her company. She should take that as a compliment, especially as this was only their second meeting.

She lay next to him feeling content and just a little smug. She had proved she wasn't the timid girl he might remember. She had turned him on, and she was sure he wasn't going to forget that in a hurry. Okay, he has sex with different women every day but Mia suspected it wasn't usually like this.

What next? This session had been intense but short, they still had plenty of time in the room, she was here with her fantasy man and she was still fully dressed. How long could he sleep? Mia touched his face very gently, and his eyes blinked a couple of times then opened with a start he stared at her with a look of panic on his face.

"I'm so sorry."

"Why?"

"I don't know how I could fall asleep when I'm here with you."

"It's okay. It was just a few minutes."

"I don't want to waste minutes with you, and you certainly haven't come here for a man to fall asleep with you."

"Don't worry we've plenty of time."

He shivered.

"You're getting cold, here get under the blanket." She pulled the covers up around him, but she didn't get under. Fully dressed and still hot she stood up next to him and proceeded to remove her clothes. She didn't just take them off as she would at home. In her year of study she had read about strip tease, burlesque and peepshows, she had studied to so that she could be in control, set the pace, set the tone at times like this. Now she was able to put her educational theory into practice.

She made eye contact with her man, inviting him to watch as very slowly buttons were undone, sleeves slipped from shoulders, and the graceful moves were a combination of suggestive gestures and yet at the same time innocent.

She lifted up her skirt to unhook the stockings from the suspenders, giving him a clear view of her pussy and legs. She replaced her foot on the floor, seemingly adopting a change of plan. She undid the buttons on the pinafore dress and slipped it off, so she was standing in just her stockings and bright red blouse, which just barely covered her pussy.

Enjoying his eyes on her, she decided to show off a little and keep his interest. She lifted the blouse just an inch or two and stroked the around the top of her thighs, lips and mound.

"If you could do anything you wanted, in the next hour, here with me, what would it be?" she asked.

Rayfe took a deep breath.

Her show, his nap they both helped. Every part of him was springing back to life, fast.

"I'd fuck you?"

"Because you think I want to or because it's what you want to do?"

"I hope it's what you want because it is definitely what I want to do."

Mia smiled, this was already the best session she had ever had with any of the men. He was right, she thought, there is a connection here between us. She couldn't quite explain it, but this man was different to all the others. There was an attraction. There was chemistry.

"Do it then, fuck me how you want to."

"Come closer," Rayfe threw back the covers and stood up in one sleek movement. When she moved closer to him and he unbuttoned her blouse. As his hands worked down the red silk, his eyes lingered on her breasts captured in her bra. The blouse dropped from her shoulders. She was aware of his great height, he stood at perhaps twelve inches taller than she did, as he straightened, and his hands at the end of long arms easily reached around to unhook her bra.

"If you want to know what I want, I want to fuck you on this bed. You at the edge here and me standing up, but I only want to do that if you want it too."

The words liquified something inside her, turning to a mellifluous flow in her cunt. That is what he wanted to do, and he cared enough about whether she wanted it too. Right now, their desires were in unison.

Without answering, she got on the bed and knelt down on all fours.

"Not that way, on your back please."

"Whatever you want," she replied, a little surprised.

"I'll get a condom, you get comfortable."

She was ready for him when he entered just a moment later, and she had to let out a moan of delight at the feeling of being filled by that lovely big cock. He held on to her hips, and he moved in, burying deep inside her. Thrusting, the rhythm slow at first but as their breathing became shallower and swifter, the fucking became deeper, faster. It had never felt like this before; it was good with all the others at a physical level, but this was something else. Mia came on his cock, her pussy pulsating, clamping and squeezing.

His jerking thrusts suggested he came too when she did.

A session with your paid-for lover will inevitably come to an end, with no future obligation. If Mia wanted more, she was going to have to do something about it. She could book him again.

&&&

"The primary function of West Beach is to enable reproduction. The success of the secondary function is what our jobs are all about. The concubine service.

By all measures the West Beach Brothel is very successful. Obviously it is profitable. But there is something else that I wanted to talk about today.

It provides a valuable discrete service for the minority of women who have those urges. Outside these wall those women are thought of as deviants and they could go for treatment to be cured of that perversion.

But I, for one, am glad those perverts find their way here.

Not just because they line our pockets with gold.

But because without them I wonder how we would control and contain these men. What would they do all day?

This is something that the anti-Brothel and anti-men protesters cannot address. They don't know any men."

Extract: Notes for speech to WB Councilors
Dr Walsh

Chapter Four

Artemis

Artemis looked mysterious, standing alone, isolated in the wasteland of derelict buildings. Once bustling shops that were boarded up long ago now stripped to brick and concrete shells, exposed to the elements with boarding removed for firewood. Everything that could be used, recycled or burned had been taken, and all that remained were the haunting skeleton reminders of the once lively businesses. It felt like a dangerous neighborhood. It probably wasn't. Remote rural areas were lawless, but The Capital was not a dangerous place, and this was still The Capital. Due to its isolation, if anywhere felt like it should be a no-go area it was the street on which Artemis stood, like a sole survivor.

Many parts of suburbia looked like this. With the population decimated and the workforce obliterated by the pandemic seventy years ago, acres of commercial and residential bricks and mortar were abandoned, looted and left to decay. At first the survivors had spread out to live in the empty buildings, the apocalyptic event apparently gave them the opportunity to better themselves as large and luxurious properties, furniture and material goods sat unused and available. Individual women took up residence in mansions and five-story townhouses with more toilets than bedrooms, however, just as quickly they moved out again. It was completely impractical to maintain such a lifestyle, such a home after most people died.

Within only two years humanity was reduced to a tiny fractions of its former numbers. A cull of biblical proportions that left towns and cities abandoned as the survivors flocked together in The Capital.

In a world where life was hard for most, Artemis was a thriving store providing for people's desire for luxuries rather than necessities.

Ten years ago the serendipitous discovery of Artemis resulted in a long and fruitful relationship without which Mia may never have visited West Beach, never discovered her inner seductress and never met Rayfe.

From the street, it was impossible to imagine what was inside the labyrinthine layout of the store. Clothes were at the front, vintage and antique clothing, originals and faux. Luxurious textiles, deep colors, Victorian and Edwardian designs from the old era hung on rails and were displayed on mannequins. Many elegant, detailed and beautiful garments that were often overly complicated to wear. No wonder these fashions didn't last. The clothing became more exotic as one progressed further into to the shop. Mia could lose herself surrounded by corsets, silk, leather, kinky styles and fetish fabrics. The Aladdin's cave of cloth that decorated the ground floor made her feel sensual and sexual. Like many women, Mia visited Artemis many times before moving beyond that first level.

The door to the stairs only became apparent after Mia had become a frequent visitor to the store. It was as if it hadn't been there before. It stood open, beckoning her to explore the depths, but it was also forbidding. A familiar member of staff nodded that it was OK to go down, it wasn't a staff only area, but perhaps that door had been shut before. Since then the basement drew her every time.

Books secreted deep in her bag, three old books, were returned to the basement book department on every visit, for a twenty percent discount on three new books. Not new, very old, most publications predated Matriarchy, being at least seventy years old and more. The old books were just new to this customer. The discount was not the driving motivation for Mia to return them; the fear of someone discovering a hoard of hetero romance books written pre and post Matriarchy in her home, however, was. Romance, sizzling erotic romance with male heroes, knights in shining armor, men who saved the day, the good guys and the bad boys. Mia enjoyed reading about them all and the women who loved them, she enjoyed the seduction and the sex. The sex in hot and hotter detail and the more explicit, the better.

Mia wouldn't want her mum, or her sister or her work colleagues to stumble on these books in her home, skim through the pages and read some of what was written. What would they think of her? She felt she could just about get away with owning three without appearing to be a pervy weirdo, if the worse was to happen, and her secret book stash was discovered. Just three books could be justified by an acceptable level of curiosity. Three doesn't suggest unhealthy obsession, or she could even claim they were a gift acquired as a risqué joke, albeit one in bad taste.

The basement was vast, Artemis was vast, but the basement seemed to extend beyond the footprint of the building above. There could be many readers investigating the titles and yet still feel private, because of the layout. Books were set out in small cul de sacs with the bookshelves forming floor to ceiling walls.

There wasn't just taboo erotic fiction down there, although there was a lot of it. There were also sweet romance, books written both before and after Matriarchy focusing on the loving and sisterly relationships between women. Steamy sexy lesbian stories possibly made up the majority of the basement's offerings. Being a lesbian was acceptable, although discretion was expected. Being interested in men was shocking, maybe society's biggest taboo.

If you ran into someone you know she wouldn't be able to tell whether you were looking at the layer of taboo man-loving fiction or aiming to buy a sweet story of sisterly friendship. The books were not in separate sections as they were in any other library or bookshop. They were layered in stripes; the shelves were eight high with the most popular genres in the middle bands running all the way around the shop. Two shelves, three in some places, were dedicated to books that included a main male character and as these shelves were at eye level sandwiched between the red hot lesbian lover novels, Mia suspected that they were among the most popular books. Whereas the no-sex, no-romance books were at floor level.

The staff knew Mia by sight; sometimes they would even put things aside to show her and often she'd buy those things. They would slip her details of things that may be of interest. It was in this way that she found out about the services of West Beach, advertised on a little flier, discreetly slipped inside a new purchase. She found out about the adult film club in the same way.

The basement wasn't the primary draw of the building today. Mia had brought the books to exchange mostly out of habit and wouldn't have bothered making the journey just for new reading material. A need for a new seduction outfit bought Artemis to her mind and here she was. There was a deal with the clothing that was similar to the books. Clothes don't last as well as books. Many of the clothes weren't genuine originals but lower quality reproductions that still served a purpose. Whether they were very old or very modern, these outfits weren't the sort of thing Mia would wear often so being able to buy, wear and return was a great offer.

She had a particular type of outfit in mind, one with tassels, lacy frills, garters, stockings, a costume really. With hair and makeup to complete the appearance, she would be transformed into a seventeenth-century Parisian burlesque performer. Rayfe wouldn't recognize her as the same woman. It should be fun, sexy and blow his mind.

&&&

"The Boundary of The Capital City are

reaffirmed. They remain unchanged. All women within and entering the Capital agree to abide by the laws of Matriarchy within this boundary."

Extract from The Capital Ordinance dated the year 63M.

Chapter Five

Another Appointment

"Rise and shine boys, you're missing the morning." The voice sounded too alert for the time of day.

Jay's head appeared over the edge of his top bunk, "The problem is with you Zand; you don't grasp basic science."

"Science?" queried Rayfe. *Science at this time in the morning! Jay, what goes on in your head?*

"It's spring, the sun is up earlier, it doesn't mean we have to be." Jay pulled the covers up over his head.

"If we're going to be on top then Zander's Dream Team has got to be up early."

"I've no trouble getting up any time," replied Jay, creating a blanket wigwam in the center of his bed, over his crotch, to illustrate his double entendre.

"I'm not going to make any of the obvious

comments that go with being on top." Unable to see what Jay was up to but with a mind in equally tuned into smutty thoughts, Paul joined in the banter from his cot on the bottom bunk.

"Zee, the kids, are obviously leaving it to me to tell you, yet again, we are not calling ourselves Zander's Dream Team. That's in your dreams." Rayfe thought he could hear sniggers from the other beds. "Jay, the past few days waking up to your cheerful face has made me realize why we don't actually sleep with the clients."

"How so?" Jay sat up, his hair in clumps and going in all directions.

"Have you seen yourself in the mirror when you first get up?" said Rayfe.

"If you deliberately tried to do that to your hair it would never work," Zander said chuckling along with Rayfe.

Jay laughed too and hung over the edge of the bed so Paul could appreciate the effect they were discussing, albeit an upside down version.

"You are hardly in a position to talk Zander, with your ponytail," Paul observed.

"Rumor has it I will lose all my strength if anyone cuts off my hair," Zander joked. "Oh no. No ideas everyone! I don't want to wake up one day with a new haircut, so practical jokes in E12 are banned," he added, wagging his finger for added effect.

"You going to tell them the real secret behind your long locks?" prompted Rayfe. Due to their longevity as roommates, they seemed to know everything about each other.

"Yeah tell us all your secrets, now we're all awake. By the way, thanks for that team leader," Jay was climbing out of his bunk, the day was starting for him.

"The women love it, long hair I mean, and you never see me with bed hair," said Zander, who tied and twisted it into some sort of head sculpture for sleeping.

"That's because we've never seen you get up in the morning, yet," Jay retorted. "What time of the middle of the night is it that you get up for a morning jog?"

"I can confirm Zee looks as lovely when he wakes up as when he is about to go see a client," Rayfe said earnestly. "It's just the rest of the time he could do with improvement."

"Hey, I thought you were my friend Rayfe. Is that anyway to treat me when I bring good news?"

"Good news for who?" asked Paul.

"For everyone, you've all got appointments today, one to ones for everyone."

"I'm booked most days, so that's not news it's just routine," grumbled Rayfe.

"It's good news for the team that the youngsters have got clients. You know how the younger ones are booked less than us grown men."

In the few days that they had been sharing the room Rayfe and Jay became used to being the parent figures of the group; affectionately referring to their younger friends as the kids. There were clearly two camps within room E12. Zander and Rayfe had been at West Beach for so long that memories of their life before it were vague and distant. Jay and Paul were both young and relative newcomers, so living and working here was still novel.

The way of life wasn't so dissimilar to life in the male units from where they came, communal domestic chores, group accommodation and a lack of privacy. At all the units, men were protected by female guards from the dangers that lay outside. The big differences being that West Beach was home for adults only. It was the only unit where sex with women constituted the work and semen was collected for preservation. At West Beach, there was also a very different atmosphere that couldn't only be due to the better facilities; though it did feel like the men here lived in luxury in comparison to the shabby existence they had known before.

"Fair point and I do hate leaving them without a babysitter," Rayfe joked.

"Rayfe you have got Mia. According to the record card she only saw you five days ago so you must have made an impression." Zander didn't pause for a reaction he didn't know this news was important so he carried on talking.

Rayfe stopped listening, stunned to hear who had booked him again and so soon. It was more than he dared to hope for after the last session. Much as he wanted to see her again he hadn't expected she would want to see him so he had been trying to forget it, which wasn't easy.

"Jay, you've got Stephanie, you've seen her a few times about once a month."

"Oh Stephanie, that's good, she's good."

"Paul, have you done any one on ones yet?"

"A few," Paul replied.

"You've got Kerry. She's new for you; I've seen her a few times. She has been visiting here for years but doesn't normally see someone as young as you. Her tastes are mainstream, as far as I know, but who knows what you might do with her."

"Feel free to tell us details later Paul," Jay said with a cheeky grin and his hand on his crotch.

Paul got out of bed, in the confined space of the room this placed him face to face with Jay.

"I'll save some stories for you, Jay," Paul paused, "and you save something for me."

***

"Minetta, I've got an important date for your diary and I'm afraid it will require diverting some of your team from their current projects." It was only at West Beach that Mia used a shortened version of her given name. She looked up to see the stout figure of Professor Francis Johnston, the owner of Exlabs and her boss, closing the door behind her as she entered the room.

"Have you got time for me to tell you about it now?" It appeared Mia had little choice as Johnston was already sitting down and getting comfortable.

"Yes of course." She made a show of closing the folder on her desk and placed it on top of a report she had yet to read. "Microbiology and Bio-fuel" was compulsory reading for her current project, but Mia had struggled to get past the Executive Summary. *It is not as if I was doing anything important.*

She had been struggling to be productive for the past few days, since seeing Rayfe. She couldn't get her daydreams under control but her boss sitting in her office gave her impetus to focus.

"The government is arranging an emergency summit to share scientific knowledge about the population problem. We have about six weeks to prepare papers for submission, they will be distributed prior to the event. I'm sure I don't need to tell you, but this could be an opportunity to increase our funding, boost our team and get approval for more research. So, we need to be clear on what we would like to get out of this."

"I understand. This is a high priority, and we should drop everything to get this done," Mia observed.

"That is precisely it." Johnston nodded in agreement.

"Why come to me, though?"

"It is a prime issue for a biochemist."

"Fertility isn't something I know much about whereas in other departments you employ experts in it. Fuel is a pressing problem too."

"I thought the issue could benefit from your fresh eyes. You are bright enough to master the published material within a short time and I would like your team to review everything we know, put it together, identify what we don't know," Johnston explained.

"We know what we know. We know there is widespread infertility amongst men and women and for all live births the ratio of boys to girls is low." Mia took a deep breath before continuing but tried to keep her voice steady and even, the words had to be said. "We know most of the population also have a depressed or non-existent sex drive."

Johnston didn't seem to notice the temperature rise in the room or that Mia's face flushed, she suddenly felt so warm. Without batting an eyelid, Mia hoped she'd got away with it.

"Yes, those assumptions are well-known, they've been around for seventy years, since the pandemic but are they groundless assumptions? I want you look at as much information as possible and see if these assumptions that still hold true. What is the latest research? What does the most recent data tell us?"

"Lots of background information gathering," Mia said. She understood what her employer required. A total review of the field, work that could take months or a year for an individual but her whole department was capable of working together to get it done within weeks. All that work would probably converge into a two-page summary, including footnotes.

"Yes," said Johnston, the normally stoic woman was leaning forward in her chair, animated and excited. "Background information that could give us a clue as to new avenues for exploration. Perhaps something missed, and when they give out the funding for it, which they will, Exlabs wants a good claim on it. Rarely does such a tremendous opportunity come our way. There will be other scientific teams there, using different data sets and with their goals."

"We also need to anticipate what cures or possible treatments other labs might be working on or might suggest. Do you know who else has been invited to participate?" Mia asked.

"I'll pass you the list with the full information package when it arrives. I have nothing in writing about it; I have only been told verbally by Kerry McCoy."

"How is her name familiar?" asked Mia.

"She's the government's chief science adviser. You must know her?"

"I know of her, yes now you've reminded me. Science is a small community, of course, but I've never worked with her," said Mia. "We'll try to anticipate what proposals the competition might come up with so that we have counter arguments at the ready if a funding battle arises."

"Good, that's what I like to hear," said the company owner. "Keep your ear to the ground and do some lateral thinking based on what we know about the competition."

"I will."

"It won't be just scientists at the summit. There will be statisticians doing population modeling. The government believe there is a real question mark over our future."

"In what way? There are enough men alive to repopulate."

"We know that but the government aren't so sure. They are getting nervous, even panicking. There is so much fighting among the factions from all sides. Some of them want to eliminate all infertile men, en masse, claiming they are a drain on limited resources. Others believe there is a population crisis and demand the government does something about it. A powerful minority want to eliminate men from the creation loop altogether."

Scientists had developed a few techniques for reproduction using only female eggs before the pandemic. The research continued with animal experimentation under the Matriarchy but it remained unlicensed, not yet accepted as a legitimate means for human reproduction. It was controversial and yet the very idea of it was popular among the masses. It wasn't popular among scientists, however, except for those who stood to gain financially if this controversial process were to be approved. To date, however, such approaches weren't sanctioned but blessed only with meager research grants to keep the techniques on the back burner, presumably ready should an emergency requiring new methods arise in the future.

"It sounds horrific. I can't believe women are considering genocide," Mia shuddered.

"I'm not sure anyone is suggesting we systematically kill them off but I think many would be happy to let men die out. If certain techniques become the way we repopulate there could be a future without men and a reproduction process that only produces double X chromosome offspring. If and when unforeseen side effects come to light it will be too late to go back to nature."

"Tampering with nature, with unpredictable results, sounds just like the experiments that led to this crisis in the first place."

Numerous Ethics Committees concurred that in principle reproduction should continue as nature designed it involving a female egg and male seed. To create a generation of women in any other way was asking for trouble in the future. Among the intelligentsia, the argument was clear. It was tampering with science beyond reason that had led to the pandemic, the artificially created virus had almost destroyed the human race seven decades earlier.

Popular opinion among the less educated masses, however, was quite different. There was always an enthusiastic reception to the idea of taking men out of the reproductive loop altogether. In school, girls learned men were the instigators behind everything bad that had ever happened, they were egomaniacs, responsible for all sorts of atrocities prior to the pandemic. The Matriarchal system removed men from all positions of power in society and naturally many women questioned the desirability of the involvement of male genes in producing their daughters. The seventy years of Matriarchy had engendered an exclusively female society that was fearful and resentful of men.

"They are extremists but these minorities can become popular when they whip up resentment against a common enemy, the enemy being men. They argue that men live in luxury at the expense of women while poorer women are struggling to survive." Johnston sat back in her chair, relaxing a little as the discussion moved from specifics to do with her business on to general society.

"Madness. What do they think we'd do without men?" Mia asked. She leaned across her desk, feeling angry and frustrated by the ignorance of many.

"I think some might want to keep the sperm bank and just a few donor men, men would be breed for that purpose and presumably only allowed to live if they were producing good enough seed."

"No. It is barbaric." Mia was shaking her head. "I was thinking more about the need for a diverse gene pool, reducing the number of donors is dangerous."

"Fortunately the women that matter agree with you on both accounts, currently. It is barbaric, and we do need a diverse gene pool."

"Anyway, we've always been told men's units fund themselves and don't take resources from us." Mia had a good understanding of how that funding worked. The sessions she had been paying for were not cheap; only her well-paid senior position and her frugal lifestyle enabled her to afford such frequent visits to West Beach.

"All the units, but for West Beach, are in far-flung remote places. If those militants turn to terrorism West Beach is the only one they could get to, most worryingly because it is the center for fertility. They could bomb it, burn it down, kill all the fertile men and destroy the sperm bank in just one senseless action."

"Crazy." Mia shook her head again and her eyes focused on the wooden grain of the desk. "Without a doubt we need to be proposing a second sperm bank at a more distant and secure location."

"Good, jot that down and put it in your report for my review." Johnston stood up indicating the meeting was over. "The finance investigation is taking place immediately following the science summit, and I'm sure that's deliberate."

"You mentioned extremists from all sides, what other viewpoints do you think the leaders will have to consider?" With her personal interest in the subject Mia wanted be clear what options might be considered for the future of mankind. The world without men seemed awful on many levels.

"There are those who want men to be integrated into society, as if that would work. That point of view isn't popular and I can't see it gaining ground."

"If we are successful in raising the male birth rate, which will be good for increasing population size and making sure people don't die out, what exactly will we do with the extra men? Should we build more men's units? Divide the land mass in half so they get their own country?" Mia hadn't given much thought to this before, as there had never been any imminent chance of a rise in the number of men.

"Precisely the questions the government need to consider. Will there be an exponential population boom and will we have sufficient natural resources or will there be shortages and famine? The moralists aren't addressing these details; they only argue that men are people too."

"What do you think?" Mia asked her boss who by now had her hand on the door handle.

"I'm a scientist so I prefer to reserve my judgment until I've seen more accurate and up to date data."

"No moral or gut feelings?"

"Honestly, I'm glad I'm not a politician and having to walk through these minefields." Johnston let go of the door handle to give Mia her attention. "What about you, what are your views?"

"I'm not sure, either. They are human so they should be protected and treated with respect but, like you, I wouldn't want to have to come up with a solution to the political problems."

"You should go over to West Beach, you haven't been there have you?"

"No." Mia gasped and practically spat out her hasty reply.

"You don't need to be scared, you are unlikely to come across a man in the science and fertility wing." Fortunately, Johnston seemed to interpret Mia's reaction as revulsion at the thought of being in that place. "I'd like you to meet up with the medical team over there, they are working on fertility and they are the main experts on the subject. Just gather background information, they have always been very accommodating to our requests before."

Mia was aware that there was a program for scientists and technical staff to gain work experience at the West Beach science wing but her area of expertise wasn't fertility. There had been no reason for her to visit in a professional capacity before.

DEVIANT

&&&

"Our mothers, sisters and daughters are dying and we cry for their loss.

We know who to blame. The scum. The rapists.

It is karma that they were most heavily hit by the disease.

That most men have died because of experiments done by men, creating chemical weapons to make men rich.

Many women want to protect those scum that remain alive. The proposal to set up the new state called Matriarchy includes the protection of men as one of its principles.

We don't need another state to replace patriarchy. With all the men gone the problem itself is gone...."

Extract from a pamphlet entitled "Men Must Pay" by the The Daughters of Scum published two years into the pandemic and shortly before the Matriarch Ordinances.

The Daughter of Scum were inspired by twentieth century radicals including Valerie Solanas, the author of SCUM Manifesto. SCUM, the Society for Cutting Up Men.

Chapter Six

Used

Mia arrived early for the session again so that she could change into something considerably sexier and prepare mentally. She had become a skilled seductress and lover through her many visits to West Beach, when she practiced the things she had read about in dusty old books. But it didn't come naturally. She carried a whole lot of mental hang-ups after a lifetime of exposure to anti-male, anti-sexual propaganda. She used the quiet time to unlock the women she wanted to be and put the model citizen of Matriarchy inside a separate compartment.

When Rayfe arrived, he shut the door behind him and stood still just inside the room by the door looking at her as if unsure what to do next, or was he waiting for her orders?

"I'd like you to take off all of your clothes before you come any closer," Mia's confident voice broke the silence. "I want a good look at you."

She stood up so that he could fully appreciate

the effort she had made. She was wearing a short black leather skirt, black knee high boots with a black leather waistcoat just covering her lacy bra. She had brought along three optional outfits and spent some time alone dressing and parading around the room in each of them. Eventually settling on the leather suit because it had the look and feel that matched her frame of mind; dirty and unashamedly sexual.

Taking his clothes off for maximum impact was something Rayfe excelled at every time they met, and this was no exception. He pulled his T-shirt slowly over his head, revealing his taut abs. She found the mat of hairs across his chest and down his stomach mesmerizing. All of the things that defined a male body, in fact, and made it instantly recognizable as male, were the very things that turned Mia on. Other women would call her a pervert, a deviant for this very reason if only they knew. Since Matriarchy, women weren't supposed to lust after men and most didn't. Right now, she planned to revel in her deviancy and desire.

His muscles looked bigger than last week, well just five days ago. After his top, he pulled down his jeans and slipped off his shoes in one seamless swift movement, no underwear.

Her eyes drank in the full vision, the figure standing in front of Mia looked huge, a well-developed male with broad shoulders and muscular arms and legs. Then there was his cock, of course, nestled in neatly trimmed hair. It wasn't quite standing to attention but launched to a semi-erect state, it was pointing to the wall.

"Do you like what you see," he asked. It was the first thing he had said since arriving. He looked like the same man but today he was more reserved compared to their previous sessions when he had charged in talking and taking control.

"Very, nice," Mia replied. "Now, what about you? Stay there and tell me if you like what you see."

Mia undid her waistcoat and let it slip to the floor then her hands went to the zip of her skirt, and that followed. She stepped out of the heap of clothing wearing only her boots, stockings, suspenders and her bra. In total contrast to the last session when she kept her clothes on for much of the time she stood before him almost naked.

"Well?"

"Beautiful."

Good, but perhaps he says this to everyone, she thought. The challenge would be to know the genuine Rayfe and not just the actor on the job.

She had also eaten almost nothing this week. Feeling distracted, she could barely concentrate on her work and knew she couldn't continue like this. She had to get the obsession with Rayfe out of her system.

"Meet me at the bed then and make me come." It took only a few steps for them both to cover the distance between them and the bed where Mia reclined with her knees bent, feet drawn up to her rear. "Just use your fingers."

He sat between her legs, and the fingers that slipped inside her weren't too much nor too soon. She was wet, very wet, and ready for anything he could give her. She was ready and had been almost the entire time since their last session. She had found it difficult to concentrate at work and even worse when at home, she could think of nothing else but having sex with this man. Now she needed desperately and urgently to scratch the itch that had been bothering her for days. No matter he had only just arrived and she had a two-hour session booked. No matter what he thought about her impatience. She was going to come, now. Her thrusting, her moaning, and her temperature all told him to put all he had into this finger fuck, and he did. He fucked her hard and fast.

"I needed that. Here, lie down next to me," she invited, and she cuddled his firm body putting her head against his chest. "I've seen many men here, but no one has turned me on like you. I couldn't stop thinking about you after our last session."

"I thought about you too, it was amazing," he said.

Mia wondered whether these words were repeated to everyone that he met a second time.

"I loved turning you on and seeing you come," she said. "I'd like to do something like that again," she said, reaching for his cock. "If you were the client, and I was here for you what would you want?"

"Sex," he said without hesitation. "It's all sex, and I like it all but mostly I'd want to fuck you."

She smiled.

"We can do that. Do you mind if I get on top?"

She reached over for a condom and expertly rolled it down his cock. He remained still as she climbed on top of him and eased herself, wet and warm on to him. Using all the strength in her legs, she moved up and down. His arms stretched out, a hand either side of his head, their bodies were apart. He had a perfect view of her breasts in front of his face.

She felt the heat rising in her, warm liquid gushing out of her. She was close to orgasm yet again; she allowed her body to fall closer to him as she rested on her elbows and brushed her cheek against his.

"You are so sexy," she whispered in his ear.

"So are you," Rayfe replied. "I love the feeling of you on my cock, I'd love to feel your orgasm as you ride me."

When he was a fantasy, it was a pleasant, mild distraction for her at home but after their recent session, the first time they actually had sex, Mia had been driven to distraction. She couldn't sleep, couldn't concentrate. She had to see him again soon knowing that it might take a few sessions, but she had to work through this and get a grip. Even if just to reduce the numerous changes of soggy wet knickers, that were a consequence of her thoughts. At this moment she knew that getting him out of her system and moving on from this would not be happening any day soon. It was hard to imagine that her hunger for this man could ever be sated.

He was unlike any of the other men, thought Mia. His presence, his touch and his voice all stoked the fire within her. She was excited by the very sight of him and by how he looked at her. The reality of touching Rayfe, in the flesh, seemed like more than she could bear.

***

He worked his hips fast. Driving his cock up into her, he felt her orgasm. Felt the unmistakable gripping and releasing of his cock, the heat surging through them both.

It was tempting; he was so close. *No. Self-control. There will be more time later.*

Her words were as disarming as ever. *Just who*

is in control of this session?

Rayfe knew he was overly sensitive and yet when she had asked him to use his fingers alone, the implication being that he shouldn't come too soon, unlike last time. She didn't say these words, but he heard them in his head, these words stung as did the guilty feeling that he hadn't been able to shed. She encouraged him in the previous session but still the thought of ejaculation so early on bothered him. He wanted to come, and he didn't want to; this time he was pleased to demonstrate that he could hold back. He intended to stay professional throughout, especially after last week.

But when she said "I loved turning you on and seeing you come," he gulped, he knew he would have to put those thoughts out of his head to stay in control today.

Don't listen to her!

She came; Rayfe felt used, and not in a bad way. That was just how it was. He was there to provide his service in whatever way women want. This was just going to be a typical session after all.

As the orgasm waned, she kissed him, their first kiss today, their mouths fused together as one.

Mia raised her face away from his to ask, "Rayfe, would you like to see me again?"

"Of course, and do you think I could say no at a time like this?" With a woman on his swollen cock that ached to come, was she serious?

"No. OK stupid question. That would be how to spoil the moment." She leaned in for more kissing, brushed her lips against his but pulled back again. "It's just that I'm enjoying being with you now and am also thinking I wish next time could be tomorrow."

Next time can be right now. Rayfe pulled her tight to him, and they rolled across the huge bed until he was on top of her. His hips wanted to thrust to satisfy his instant needs, but his mind was in control, so he focused on the bigger reward. Two hours with this exceptionally sexy woman who was into him too. He intended to fill those hours with physical contact to take them both to the heights of ecstasy. Right now, that meant pulling out, moving his lips down her body so that she would anticipate his tongue, but she would have to wait for it. The sight of Mia, purring and writhing confirmed the wisdom of his plan.

Time picked up speed and the two hours passed far too quickly, it wasn't like this with all clients, there were days when the minutes dragged.

&&&

"We are supposed to be the lucky ones, lucky to be alive. I'm not so sure that's true. We've all been hit by devastating personal loss. Personally I've lost every man in my family, every man I've ever known or loved.

Most of the women are gone too and even though I'm surrounded by all of you survivors. I've never felt so alone.

Nothing can change that and there is no-one left alive today who caused this catastrophe.

Blaming one group or other will solve no problems and right now we need solutions."

Extract from notes for a speech prepared by a survivor speaking at a Matriarchy rally a few years after the outbreak of the pandemic.

Chapter Seven

Midsummer's Beach Party

The guards were like wallpaper. Their white and cream colored uniforms blended into the background rendering them almost invisible. Like wallpaper, they did not make eye contact or engage in conversation. They were always present, if not within sight, then nearby. Unlike wallpaper, however, they moved about and could gather in groups in the open air. Sometimes they would even carry weapons, which would be most unbecoming of wallpaper. The guards at West Beach didn't serve a merely decorative function.

Two walls of armed guards lined the beach in either direction, a distant but visible reminder nevertheless that there was always the potential for unrest. Today, the guards' presence as ever was ostensibly to protect the men from outsiders. At the top of the beach, inland beyond the sand dunes, stood the West Beach facility, with its imposing perimeter wall. The sea being the natural fourth barrier, surrounding the party on the sand. Keeping the party guests hemmed in or keeping outsiders out? Fortunately, the two movable barriers, the guards, always remained unchallenged at these events, but they were there, just in case they were needed.

"I love this time of year, the lazy days, for this reason," Zander announced to the small group gathered around the self-service drinks table, otherwise referred to as the bar. "You can't help feeling good when the evenings are as bright as midday."

"The sun is still high in the sky. Hard to believe it is almost seven o'clock," Eric said, he had been roommates with Rayfe and Zander prior to the reorganization.

"We say the same thing every year," Mick joined in. He added, "You'll have to invent some new lines for yourself Ray, if you want to join in our well-rehearsed conversations."

The guys laughed.

"As it's my first time at this particular party perhaps I'd better just watch, listen and learn," Rayfe replied.

The annual midsummer beach party was a casual affair about half the men wore shorts and T-shirts, some had bare feet, others were a little more covered up but still in casual clothes, suitable for the beach on a hot summers evening. The sand under foot and the sound of the waves breaking on the shore made for a relaxed, back to nature atmosphere, only enhanced by the subtle drumming of the musical ensemble. An assortment of percussion instruments, suitable for sandy beach conditions, was available to the four-man band.

"Coach loads of women will arrive at any minute," said another man whose name Rayfe couldn't remember. Despite being ten years in the community, it was possible to see some people very rarely and even though all the faces were familiar, he didn't know everyone.

"Coach loads?" Rayfe queried, it wasn't what he had been told.

"In your dreams! There will be fewer women than men. There are about eighty men here so there might be about forty to fifty women," Zander explained.

"These women will be frequent visitors to West Beach and they must be women who aren't afraid of being recognized by other women. Knowing that they all share this secret they are unlikely to cause trouble for each other," said Eric. He was older than Zander, and could barely have looked more different. Eric drew the short straw when hair and stature were distributed, but he was here, a testament to the fact that different women look for a variety of things in a man. The lack of hair on his head wasn't totally due to premature baldness, Eric was only forty, but he shaved his entire head instead of supporting a bald patch and a smattering of gray.

In contrast, the four men in room E12 were matched for size as if the fact that there were empty beds in the room was due to the room being inhabited by giants. The E12 residents each exceeded six foot and all had plenty of hair. Zander, with his long thick ponytail, had more than enough hair for four of them.

"Mostly it is the same women every year and

some of them will be coming just to socialize with one man, their favorite boyfriend. Others attend to flirt with all of us."

"There will be a shuttle bus if any of them want to disappear off to a private room later in the evening."

"And here they come."

A small cheer sounded from the beach as a coach slowed to a halt on the small vehicle-parking strip a hundred yards away.

The women climbed off the buses and made their way along the wooden boards that ran like bridges over the sand to the party on the beach, some stopped to remove shoes and continued in bare feet.

Rayfe scanned the crowd backwards and forwards, almost holding his breath, hoping to see a certain someone, Mia. After frequent visits for eight weeks, since mid-April, Mia had suddenly disappeared from his life. He hadn't openly acknowledged, even to himself, how much he looked forward to seeing her. How excited he was those mornings when he discovered she was his going to be one of his clients again, booked for that day. There was no logical reason for how he felt, why he would have a big smile on his face for the whole day. There were other regular clients but with her everything felt different.

The session at the beginning of June was the last time he saw her. He had no idea why, he was only entitled to see her client card on the day of her booking so there was no knowing what she was doing unless she booked him again. On the other hand, perhaps she was ill, or even dead, if so he would never know. No one would think it important to tell him.

He had no idea how to contact her or how to find her, no telephone number and no address. That isn't how things are done. Why had he never thought to question it before? Women are in control of the relationships, they hold all the power. It had never mattered to him before because it had never mattered. He'd never cared about a client before. Sure, he liked some, liked some of them a lot, but never really cared. He'd never fallen in love before. This was all different.

No sign of Mia among the crowd and, though disappointed, Rayfe was unsurprised. It would be strange for her to suddenly just show up today, unexpectedly. The women who attended had no fear of being recognized and exposed; most attending these types of gatherings did so on a regular basis and knew each other. Rayfe picked out a few familiar faces though he couldn't clearly place them, as it may have been several years ago that he had met them in a session.

He noticed Rose who he had seen as part of a foursome with Jay and Paul. He also spotted two women that he knew as lesbian performers at the erotic shows, exhibitionists, he was surprised to see them here as he had assumed they were only into putting on a show he hadn't thought they might be actually into men. He was no expert, perhaps these women were into many things and as they had never booked him before.

"I can see some of my favorite old flames," Zander whispered in Rayfe's ear. "What about you?"

"Not exactly, but there's certainly some I wouldn't say no to."

"I'm pleased to hear it, after all the moping you've been doing lately."

"Moping?"

"Yes, not exactly miserable, but very quiet and distracted. Maybe now isn't the time but if there is something on your mind mate, you can talk to me," Zander paused, "Your team leader."

"I might just do that." Rayfe surprised himself with the answer that came out before he had time to think about it.

The mid-summer's beach party was an annual event and just one of many similar events through the summer. A small and select number of women received invites to attend parties with a small group of the community's men. It was a rare opportunity to mix with like minded people, others like themselves, and to socialize with the men, dance and chat, rather than being shut away in a private room as if sex was the only thing deviant women wanted.

Many of the women considered themselves to be in relationships with the men. Rayfe reflected on this, the social events had to be carefully organized to avoid two women attending who both laid claim to the same man. Not all were interested in monogamous relationships; people like Rose were free spirited fun seekers, perhaps more like the men. The men weren't monogamous, at least none were as far as Rayfe knew.

What is the matter with me, thought Rayfe. Women become attached to one man; at least some of them do, so why shouldn't men feel that same attachment? Or do they? I guess I've not thought about it much.

Becoming attached to a woman wasn't something the men talked about either. Sure, they talked about having favorite clients but not about their emotions, not about falling in love.

A beautiful, mature woman approached the group. Zander headed straight for her.

"Clare it's good to see you, I wondered if you would make it?" They embraced with a friendly but intimate kiss on the cheek.

"Come and let me introduce you. This is Rayfe; he's my roommate, one of them. This is Eric, an ex-roommate, Cody and Mick."

"How many roommates do you have?" Clare asked looking at Rayfe.

"There are just four of us now, but the other two aren't here," Zander replied.

"I've got to ask, why is Eric your ex? Did he kick you out or was he the terrible roommate?" she broke the ice with a question that got the men chuckling.

"If only you saw the mess he makes in his room!" Nodding of heads, including Eric's, and more chuckles supported this comment.

Rayfe spent the evening of the longest day of the year feeling lonely despite mingling, being charming and the crowd of familiar and friendly faces around him. He flirted a little with Rose who asked about Paul and Jay. She gave every indication that she'd be booking the team again but made it clear she didn't have plans that involved Rayfe that evening. She enjoyed interacting with everyone at the party women and men.

Zander remained in the company of Clare for the evening. They looked very happy together, as if they were at their own private party, somehow blocking out all others to share private jokes and slow close dances. Seeing them together stirred up new feelings within Rayfe, he wished Mia was there to share the evening with him.

After the guests had departed, the men made their way back up the beach for the walk home across the sand dunes and through the grounds. It was a fair hike so ferrying people by minibus was an option but it was a lovely night for walking and getting out on to the beach was a rare treat for the men despite living so close to it. There was also a great buzz among the crowd as eighty or so men chatted, mingled and reviewed the night as they snaked their way home.

"How was your first mid-summer beach party?" Zander asked as he caught up with Rayfe.

"Just like any other beach party," Rayfe replied.

"Well I hope it's cheered you up a little."

"I didn't know I needed cheering up." Rayfe lied, so it was obvious then, he thought.

"Are you lads coming for some R and R by the pool?" asked Cody as they neared the village.

"Not for me," Zander replied. "It's been a long day and I'm still hoping to get up just after the dawn chorus."

"Why?"

"It's just what I do."

"Coming Rayfe?"

"No I'm going to find my bed, too. Goodnight."

Rayfe and Zander turned off the main trail into the tightly packed maze of single story one-room buildings that made up the village.

As they approached E12, Zander continued their conversation in a low quiet voice. "What's the matter with you?" Zander asked. "Was there a bad session with a client?"

"No."

They reached the door of the cabin and walked in. Rayfe kicked off his shoes and lay down on his bunk hoping the change of scenery would end that conversation. Paul and Jay were already in bed asleep. Rayfe was relieved that Zander suspended interrogation for the night rather than proceeding with whispers but he took it up again the following night.

&&&

"Humanity is facing a new crisis.

Men are living in hiding. Men are being murdered.

Yet at the same time we are facing a crisis of reproduction with very few babies being born and as far as we can tell most but a minority of people are fertile.

An urgent response is already being put into place. Five communities are being set up for men to live safely but separately from women. More will be set up as and when needed. These communities will be away from our established towns. And they will be fully self sufficient within three years.

Men are vital for our future and are equal citizens with women under Matriarchy.

The male communities will have the full protection of our army.

Alongside this move to protect this vulnerable group of people we will also be starting an urgent comprehensive study of fertility."

Extract from a government news bulletin sex years after the establishment of Matriarchy.

Chapter Eight

The New Clothes

Another late night in Exlabs was nothing unusual for Mia up until little over a year ago, when she found an alternative interest. Women in science worked exceptionally long hours because of their personal commitment to science. Whether their aim was to expand human knowledge, make significant advances in medicine or further their careers. It was usually some combination of the three. The scientist contributed more than they were paid for, and they were passionate about their field and highly self-motivated. The owners of Exlabs benefited from that drive.

Mia was examining the samples she had collected from West Beach that afternoon. She had dropped into the Fertility Research Unit, without an appointment, hoping to pick up some samples as she had forgotten to take them on the day of her scheduled interview. All of the senior team were out at their clinics in The Capital. With only junior students holding the fort, Mia was encouraged to help herself and she selected random samples from the storeroom.

Using the various techniques and equipment she had at Exlabs, she checked and rechecked repeatedly. Contrary to expectation, all of the semen samples seem to have a high number of male sperm. The ratio might not have been fifty-fifty but close to it, perhaps forty sixty. Whereas the rate of male births would have suggested a ratio that was far worse. There had to be an explanation. A reason the birthrate was so low. Even if they were unable to travel the entire distance to reach the egg that explanation didn't hold for assisted conception. Various techniques were available such as intracytoplasmic sperm injection, whereby the sperm had no distance to travel but were injected into the egg.

Of course, miscarriages and stillbirths may make a difference. It could be that male foetuses were weak, not as robust and less likely to survive the full term compared to females. It could also be something about these particular sperm samples, though what remained unclear. Mia had selected the specimens at random. Although only small in number, it didn't seem likely that she could have picked the only semen from the entire store that was rich in the potential for creating male life.

Mia worked around the clock, carrying out tests and considering possibilities.

The results begged some questions. If the

sperm that can produce XY chromosome babies, males, is available in plentiful supply, why haven't the fertility scientists been selectively using it? Why not selectively choose the sperm, choose the donor and raise the number of boy babies?

Mia had all of her results from the samples by midnight, but she kept working, seeking a rational explanation as to why the result were in direct contradiction to what she expected. There had to be an alternative way of interpreting the data, and explanation, something she had missed. Everyone "knew" most babies are girls, there had to be a reason.

It was the height of summer and only truly dark for a few hours, this helped to trick her body into finding extra energy as she worked through the night. By about six in the morning, she decided to lie on the couch in the staff room for a while.

"I know you're not in early, Mia. You're in late, you never went home!"

***

Rudely awoken by a colleague after less than an hour of sleep she was persuaded to leave for her bed. Where she might get some more sleep. The substantial stash of old publications that she had taken for background reading on reproduction, and was now forming a mountain in the center of her home, provided a bigger incentive to go than a mere rest. Many of those documents she had found buried in the archives predated the pandemic. She hoped they would hold answers.

We all make mistakes, and we have the experience of being unable to see the very thing that is in front of our face. Such as hunting all around the house for keys, only to find they are on the key rack. Little mistakes in everyday life with no consequence are one thing but to risk ridicule or worse at work in front of peers is another. Mia couldn't afford to take any risks with her career. She'd stormed up the scientific ladder, reaching heights not normally achieved by someone of her age, and with a whole team answering to her. They say the higher you climb, the harder the fall and Mia didn't intend to get hurt.

Was she simply not seeing something obvious that everyone else could see and that would be extremely embarrassing if she were to share her thoughts with her colleagues?

Rather than discuss evidence that appeared to fly in the face of conventional wisdom, Mia naturally tried to keep such thoughts to herself. Instead, her approach was to investigate the problem from every angle in the assumption that she was wrong and common sense was right.

This must be how numerous scientists felt when they reached conclusions that were in contradiction to the way everyone else understood the world. When Copernicus and others deduced the world is round, despite the way we all experience it on a daily basis, as flat. When Hubble discovered the universe was expanding regardless of the laws of gravity. Or, when mercury was found to be a toxic poison, not the medical panacea that it was once considered to be.

Mia had a very uneasy feeling about the information her team had been collecting about the reasons and possible remedies for the low birth rate of males. Everyone knew there was an event that changed the human race and within two years most of the population was dead. This event, the pandemic, was due to a virus that spread throughout the world and no one was left untouched. Among the survivors human DNA was altered. Widespread infertility and low birth rate were the long term consequences but also a very low number of male births compared to the number of girls that were born. Worryingly low, so low that it would be difficult to sustain the population. Extinction was on the cards.

The pandemic started just over seventy years ago. Since that time, everyone lived with the knowledge that there were few male births and that the state must protect men for their important role in replenishing the sperm banks. Worryingly most men are infertile, so the treasure of men is even more valuable. This was all common knowledge.

Through the information gathering process, initiated to verify the common knowledge, Mia had the horrible feeling that she had stumbled across at least one contradiction, if not many. The evidence didn't support the facts, or the facts failed to stack up in the way expected by common knowledge. Something was wrong. Perhaps that something was just Mia making a big career-breaking mistake. Perhaps she was distracted by her secret visits to West Beach and her infatuation.

Mia felt cross with herself. She needed a clear head, to think. And having a clear head seemed to be a distant memory from the time before she first met Rayfe.

****

"I don't want to be still sharing a dorm with random guys when I'm fifty, no offense to you, Zander and I'd like to be able to choose my clients." What was the matter with him? Rayfe couldn't explain his melancholy feeling. He had a great time with today's client. Great? It was just normal, very much like any other. The woman had the satisfaction she wanted, and lots of it. The session pretty much followed his familiar formula. She said she wanted to see him again soon, great another booking, another regular.

So why was he feeling just a little bit shit?

"I know what you mean. It's all novel and fun when you're new here, for the first few years, but that novelty wore off for me too. Wore off a long time ago." Zander was in his PJs changed for sleep and lying in his bed. He turned on his side to face Rayfe. "What's on your mind mate?"

"What do you mean?" Rayfe was also lying on his bed.

"That look on your face isn't the look of a man resting after a long day and good sex. Did something happen?"

"No, it was fine. It's not that at all," Rayfe replied. "Can I ask you a question, Zee?" He didn't look his friend in the face but stared at the bed covers he was absent-mindedly rolling in his hands.

"Sure."

"Do you ever get fed up with fucking all these strangers and not getting to know any of them?"

"Mostly they are not strangers. I've been seeing some of them for ten years or more."

"But you don't see them out of those rooms, just doing everyday things like jogging or eating."

"I see women like Clare at the social events, there are lots of these for older clients and, therefore, for the older men that they like to book. Apart from that I don't think about the impossible, I just want to achieve what is possible," Zander replied. After a moment of silence he continued. "Why? Is this a general observation of yours or have you fallen in love?"

"No, I'm not in love with a client! It's stupid. I wasn't thinking of it like that," Rayfe couldn't help laughing. That wasn't what he was thinking, but his feelings for Mia were a big part of the turmoil inside of him. "Although, why not fall in love with a woman? Is it right that we have to live separately from them?"

"It's not really up to us to choose. You know that. Here we are safe, out there we aren't safe, you know that. Here we can work together and have a good life, out there, on our own, we'd have no job, no community. We might well starve if crazy, weapon-wielding vigilantes don't get us first,"

Zander summed up the world as all men knew it. Brought up in the men's units, having minimal contact with the opposite sex, through education men learned to fear women. They were mostly harmless but the minority of militant extremists who hated men were large enough in number that men were outnumbered. Living together and protected by trained guards was the only way men could survive.

"Well, do you ever feel used by the clients?"

"Oh Rayfe, I'd like to hear you ask Jay that one," Zander said with a chuckle. Zander and Rayfe were alone as their roommates were out late. "Are they using us are we using them? Does the concept of using something apply?"

"I've got overly attached to one of my clients, which has made me question the whole way we live here. She has all the power to book me or not and my time with her is controlled. I can't just hang out with her, in the same way that I would with you guys. I can't visit her or even contact her." Rayfe laid out his issues as they applied to him. He specifically wanted the older man's opinion, as he knew Zander and the older guys not only had more experience but frequently saw the same regular clients over years. "What do you think about that Zander?"

"What does she say about it?"

"I've not talked about it with her. Sometimes I think the feelings might be mutual, and sometimes I think it is in my head. But you know that's not the point. I might never see that woman again, but now the question is in my mind. What control do we have over our lives, what choices can we make."

"If it is about one woman you should talk about it with her. You can contact her you know," Zander replied.

"No, I didn't know. How?"

"You can write letters and phone her at home, but you have to arrange it with her when she is here. She has to give permission as it might not suit her to get letters and phone calls from a man," Zander said. "You know some of the women do consider the men to be their boyfriends, and they come to parties and book all night sessions with them. Some of the men feel the same way, but just don't talk about it. It sounds to me that you might feel that way because this relationship is still new. You want more time with the woman than you actually get but over time this could transform into a comfortable arrangement. Enjoy what you've got, life could be a lot worse," said Zander.

Rayfe had not seen Mia for three weeks, and he was counting the days.

***

The first problem was that if you went back to pre-Matriarchy, before the pandemic, scientists and fertility experts were already able to determine gender at conception with ease. Sperm sorting, developed more than a century earlier, seemed to be no longer used and long forgotten. When more than three-quarters of the population is wiped out overnight of course much specialist knowledge will be lost, especially that which was rarely used.

It may well have been that everyone involved in this work died in the pandemic as the scale of it was phenomenal and, indeed, lots of expertise was lost. The research papers were still there, however, lying at the back of libraries, in the archives, untouched for seven decades. If Mia could find them so easily then surely the fertility experts working in the field were aware of them. This one technique alone could change the world. Individual sperm could be isolated, gender identified and male babies produced to order. All babies born next year could be male; there could be a huge program to do that.

If it was so easy, it does beg the question why no one had rediscovered this in the past seventy years. Either discovered these papers or made the breakthrough, reinvent these techniques when the male birth rate was the single biggest problem facing humanity. Mia had never worked on the fertility issue before, and she was concerned that perhaps some part of the jigsaw was missing.

She also had an uneasy feeling about West Beach. Everything was located there, like having all our eggs in one basket. The fertile men, the sperm bank, the fertility doctors and fertility researchers, all based in one location and all with a stake in the status quo. If men were not in short supply, there would be less of a reliance on the sperm bank and the fertility scientists.

The spectacularly simple solution reminded Mia of the children's story The Queen's New

Clothes.

A wealthy monarch had the wool pulled over her eyes by cunning merchants who won a lucrative contract to provide her with a wardrobe of clothes made from the finest nano thread. A thread that was so expensive and exquisite, she would be the envy of all. Everyone who was anyone wanted nano clothing. When the orders were fulfilled, it turned out, of course, that the cloth was so sheer it was like wearing nothing at all. It was a great seller, nevertheless, because everyone bought into the idea of modern technology.

The nano cloth was a great success for the company that designed, made and sold the clothes fashioned from because they actually had another business that profited very well. Their main income was from lingerie. Women buying the new clothes knew other people could see their underwear, they were not completely gullible! So they bought tons of gorgeous lingerie, complete body suits of the stuff, and, of course, never wore the same undergarment two days in a row.

The Queen's New Clothes was just a kid's story, but it came to Mia's mind now. To what extent did the team at West Beach benefit from the current situation. All the women involved in the fertility set up, from those running the men's units, to the scientists and medical doctors involved in reproduction, they all profited from the shortage of men. If the male birth-rate problem were solved those researchers, and the fertility doctors would be largely out of a job. Not true, they could work in other scientific roles, and the medics could continue in the gynaecology and fertility field.

Similarly, if there were a solution to the population problem would they need West Beach at all? The men were there primarily to stock the sperm banks. Take away the sperm bank and then all that is left is a brothel, just as the protesters had complained.

Would men continue to live in Men's Units, however, if instead of being a protected minority they made up around half the human population? That would not make sense, and it might not be economically viable either.

There were big political questions here, and Mia was not a politician. These are not questions she could discuss with others without double and triple checking her information. What she wanted to recommend was trialling the sperm sorting techniques. Taking batches of seamen, sorting it using the methods she had read about and then tracking it through to conception and birth.

Many scientific teams were looking at the fertility and population problem in the run-up to the summit but for the most part women assumed the background assumptions are accurate. Teams were looking for solutions based on samples and data provided by West Beach. That single unit held the key to everything, all the samples, all the data and most of the research. The big question was whether West Beach could be trusted?

A conspiracy theory was not just forming in Mia's mind but jumping up and down refusing to be ignored. With no independent checks on the

West Beach unit, who can say whether or not sorting and discarding sperm had happened for decades. But done in such a way as to maintain the imbalance artificially, a situation that benefited West Beach. The more she thought about it the more she suspected the senior scientific team would be able to implement such a sorting system without the junior technicians even realizing that it was happening. When the juniors were left in charge, they were oblivious to the implication of an outside scientist helping herself to random samples.

Mia looked at the clock on her sitting room wall. It was late afternoon already. After a few hours sleep when she arrived home in the morning and hours looking at old research Mia needed a distraction. She had not seen Rayfe for over a week, or was it two? She had been absorbed in her work but also felt self-conscious about visiting that side of the unit within days of visiting her professional peers working at that same location.

She made the call.

"Hello, this is Member 69MF736. Is it possible to see my usual man today? OK. What about tomorrow? Booked. I will call back another time then."

When she terminated the call, she recognized the feelings of jealousy raging through her. She had always put the thought of him with other women to the back of her mind, but he was with someone tonight when Mia wished it was her. She couldn't see him tomorrow after work either. She could go in the daytime, but she didn't think she'd be able to get away from work in time. Also, she didn't like the thought of seeing him in the afternoon knowing that he would be saving something for a later client.

Damn.

Mia decided to open some wine and put work out of her mind. She probably needed a fresh start on the data tomorrow.

&&&

"Men are driven by nature to reproduce.

They have sex without feelings for their mate and often without any consideration for the well being of that person."

extract from Her-Story,
text book for school girls
published when Mia's grandmother was a child.

Chapter Nine

Clean Clothes

If you lived in a large community, that was more akin to an extended family in excess of one thousand men, the result would be a mountain of laundry. There were a lot of smelly socks and a pile of damp towels. You do not want to see the mountain of sheets and towels that require laundering at West Beach. To compound the problem the men in this community are all keen sportsmen or keep fit freaks getting through clean sports gear at a phenomenal rate. Looking good and keeping fit not only went with the job but helped to pass the empty hours.

The only sensible way to manage the laundry was to tackle it in the same way as any other chores, through community work. Take on the domestic challenges on an industrial scale with commercial equipment. All the younger men rotated through the different work sections on a regular basis: cleaning, laundry, catering, gardening and so on. The way out of the monotony of it all was to be on the leader board. Leader board names were those who bought in the greatest income to the Men's Unit, In return they could choose where they did and didn't work and what chores they did. They could get the best positions and could be supervisors or managers instead of getting their hands dirty.

In the basement of the main building, Rayfe was thinking about an ideal time in the future when he wouldn't have to fold towels. He had been doing this repetitive movement, as if on a factory assembly line for well over an hour and the backlog of towels was never ending. There would always be more towels to fold.

Music got the men through a day in the laundry with lots of dancing and singing along to familiar tunes, there were certainly worse places to work. Music and dancing, indoors, in the warm and dry, even when the weather was bad.

"Rayfe, Ray, outside world calling Ray." A hand passed in front of Rayfe's face. "I see signs of brain function. We can still save him."

"Naran, sorry what is it?" Rayfe's eyes focused on the face of the person who seemed to have been trying to get his attention for some time.

"I've been talking to you, but you are on your own planet, mate. You got to go get ready. There is a client to see you right now."

It was always a possibility that someone could drop into the unit without an appointment and pick a man at random. There were usually some men on standby for this, but a client could request someone else and today was one of those days.

The office was right at the top of the stairs, so Rayfe checked in. "Someone wants me?"

"Yes Mia, she's seen you quite a few times do

you want to look at the card to remind you?"

"No, I remember her."

"She wants lunch with you, and she says you should just go as you are."

"Looking like this and smelling of the laundry. No way!"

"Well, be quick and be casual. The kitchen is knocking up some food and getting it sent to the room in about thirty minutes."

Rayfe dashed to his room, grabbed some clean jeans and a T-shirt and then ran to the nearest shower block. A few minutes later feeling clean and refreshed but without underwear or socks he made his way back up to the main building. He was still carrying the clothes he'd taken off. He figured he didn't have time to make the detour back to his room to dump them and pick up the forgotten items.

It was barely midday but sitting alone for thirty minutes Mia began to recognize how exhausted she felt. Not sexy, unlike on her previous visits here. Today she was wearing a brown trouser suit. She was carrying a case full of documents, and she had one open on the desk to make good use of the time, but her tired eyes were struggling to focus. She could have happily shut them and rested her head on the table. Work had taken its toll, keeping her up at night reading old research, reports from the archives and traveling to early morning meetings.

"Hi, you showered." She noticed the still wet hair and the bundle of fabric under his arms, clothes? She smiled.

"I'm glad you could come to lunch. The food is on its way. Come and sit down." She indicated towards the table covered with a white cotton tablecloth. There were two glasses and a jug of water.

"You booked me so I came though I must admit I am surprised."

"I was working in the area."

"Working in the area?" His voice was full of skepticism and the words didn't sound like they could possibly be true when they fell from his lips. West Beach was, after all, miles from anywhere even the relatively close science park where Mia worked.

The science park and West Beach were located on this stretch of coast for a reason. The remote location had benefits. There was space for expansion, the isolation offered security and yet the capital was a short distance connected by train. The only functioning train line in the country, outside the city.

"Yes, I had to come to WB for work today."

"Why?" Rayfe looked incredulous.

"I'm a scientist remember? I came to meet with a colleague in the fertility center here."

"Oh."

"I'm looking into why so few males are born. I'm preparing a paper for the government on the subject."

"And you've been too busy for the past few weeks?" Was it a question or was Rayfe finishing her sentence. It sounded like an accusation. Like he wanted an explanation as to why she had not found time to see him. Mia dismissed this idea, he only saw her as a client, he couldn't actually miss her as she missed him.

"Yes, I have been busy and so have you. You were booked when I tried to make appointments. I would have liked to see you sooner. There are a lot of things I'd like to do but...," she couldn't think of an ending. "I'd like to get to know you. The real you not the act you put on with a client."

"Mostly I think you've seen the real me. Of course, sometimes I do just do what I believe the customer wants." He was smiling, that might be the real him.

"Does the real you like me?" Mia asked.

"Yes, I like you a lot but if the truth were no, how could I possibly tell the any client that?"

"True. OK, different question, would the real you like to live in a world where men and women mix together and are not segregated?" Mia asked.

"You are asking about fantasy, why?"

"If it were possible, I'm curious to know about what men, in general, might want. What you would want?"

"Men, in general, I don't know. Most men seem happy with things as they are. Me, I'm not. If you really want the truth, I don't know whether I would like spending time with women, doing everyday things, like folding laundry and cooking but I would like to try it. I'd like to get to know a woman without her paying to have sex with me. Much as I do like the sex. Don't get me wrong!"

They both laughed, and she reached across the table to hold his hand.

"What happened to you? Why did you take over a year to decide you want to see me again, and then suddenly you are here every week?" The abruptness of the question was startling to both of them.

"I wanted to see you again as soon as I first met you, but I didn't know what I was doing, and I didn't like that feeling. You were experienced with the opposite sex and an expert in physical things. I didn't even know anything about simple stuff. I liked you, but I wanted to be your equal. When I met you again, I wanted to feel confident that I was experienced, knowledgeable and competent. Just like you. I wanted you to seduce me, of course, but I wanted to be able to seduce you too."

"I feel I should say I understand, but I don't. So what changed?" Rayfe asked.

"I read books, I watched films, and I dug out archive material on sexual relationships before the pandemic. I used those things to get an educational," Mia explained.

"It seems to have worked, you are a sexy seductress, all right. What about all the other men you booked to see?"

Mia was bewildered, how could he know. She swallowed, it had never felt right to tell him about the others as if he would be jealous even though he had no reason to be.

"When you make a booking we get to see a full list of all your previous bookings," Rayfe explained, answering her obvious surprise that was emphasized by the silent pause between them. "Unless you are the sort of person who has been visiting every week for twenty years or more. There are some like that, and then we must get about the last thirty bookings and have to ask if we'd like more information."

"Information? What do you know about the bookings?"

"Nothing really, just the date and the name of the man or men involved."

He seemed to be waiting for an answer to his earlier question, and he was not sidetracked.

"The other men were about practice and gaining experience. And," she paused, unsure how to put it into the right words.

"And?"

"And just meeting other men. Remember you

were the first and only man I'd ever met. Perhaps I was infatuated with you for that reason."

"Makes sense."

"Does it? I thought you might be jealous?"

"Why would I be jealous?"

"I don't know," Mia mumbled with embarrassment.

"I see other women for work every day. Are you jealous?" He asked the question as if the answer was obviously no, as if the idea of jealousy had never occurred to him.

"Well, yes. I'm envious that they're seeing you when I'm not, and I do feel like I'd like to keep you to myself. Does that sound crazy?" she confessed.

"Crazy? I'm not sure. It sounds new to me."

There was a knock at the door. A guard brought a selection of sandwiches, cakes and drinks. She pushed the trolley to the table where they sat in silence until she left.

"So here we are. Lunch. No sex, and I am officially at work. How do you like it?" Mia changed the subject when they were alone again.

"Not sure, I think I need to try it out for a bit longer." His expression softened as he accepted the answers to his questions. "And I like you. I'd like to try you out for a lot longer."

"Are you hungry?" she asked.

"Yes."

"Let's tuck in."

Neither of them made a move on the food, they looked at it.

"Is this the sort of food you'd usually eat?" Rayfe asked.

"Yes, why?"

"Well, it's not how we normally have it. I mean,

we have sandwiches made out of exactly the same ingredients, they've come from the same kitchen. What is different is how they're cut. Here they are many small pieces, made into a little sculpture. When we get a sandwich, it is still whole."

"I see what you mean. They are decorative, almost bite-size pieces."

"What do you mean, almost? I really could eat them in one bite if I wanted to." Rayfe picked the one off the very top of the pile, opened his mouth wide and popped it in to demonstrate.

"My sister might serve them as tapas, a Spanish-style snack. She calls tiny sandwiches pepito. She's in catering."

"Pepito, where I come from that is the word for tiny penis. Also Spanish, I think."

"Pepito, tiny penis? Why would you need to have a word for it?" Mia and Rayfe laughed together.

"Thinking about it puts me off eating them!"

"Me too. I admit I don't normally cut up sandwiches so small either. It would be nice to take you home with me so you could see."

"I'd like to see where you live."

"Would you? Do you feel you are free to leave? In the news a while ago, the governor here said that the men are not prisoners but choose to be here. Is that how you see it?" Mia asked, it was just one of many questions that had been bothering her and the conversations this lunch time seemed to be about airing concerns.

"I never think about it in those terms. I do feel free to leave, to go to another Men's Unit. I feel I'm free within here. I think of it as home and I've never thought of it as a prison, there are no locks on the doors. There is nothing here to force me to do anything I don't want to. I do things I don't like doing, like cleaning the toilets, because it has got to be done, and we all take our turn, so the answer is yes I am free."

"But could you leave with me this afternoon?" He was a prisoner. All men are prisoners. Surely that's how they see it.

"No, but that is to do with your world, not mine. Correct me if I'm wrong but most women hate men, most blame men for destroying the world, even though we weren't alive back then. There are enough extremists and enough fear out there in your world for it to be unsafe. The world you live in is very dangerous and in here, it isn't."

"That's an interesting way of looking at it. You live on the best side of the wall, and it is the people on my side who are not free." Mia was surprised as she'd never considered that's how the men saw their situation.

"Yes, you could put it like that. Did you really see it the other way round?" Rayfe's brow was furrowed, a mixed look of amazement and confusion on his face. "Take sex, for example. Men here all do it, enjoy it, have plenty of partners. We can choose not to see a client if we want. We can talk about it with the rest of the chaps or keep that part of our lives completely private. How does that compare for women?" He already knew the answer.

"The opposite, you know that don't you? Sex is completely taboo. Some women are in lesbian relationships and that is tolerated, although women are expected to be discreet, there are no public displays of affection. As for heterosexuality, it is the ultimate taboo." Mia struggled to comprehend the new view of society. She could completely understand what Rayfe was explaining, but it went against what she'd learned her whole life: men were locked in segregated units to keep women safe.

"You've already said there are a lot of things you would like to do but cannot. I think I live on the best side of the wall. Don't you?"

"Something to think about while I chew on a pepito," Mia bit into a sandwich.

The idea of freedom is a bit of an abstract concept," Rayfe reached across the table offering her his hand. "Have you ever thought to ask whether you could live here?"

"I never thought about that." Interesting idea, must think more about that one later, she thought.

"Have you got enough background information now for your scientific investigation?"

"That's not why I'm here," Mia replied feeling hurt that he would think she was.

"Sorry. I assumed, what with the questions and no sex, and you said you're at work."

"Yes, my day job brought me here, to the fertility research unit, but I'm here with you because I like you, and I've missed you. I want to get to know you. Especially now you've asked me to come and live with you," Mia said with a smile.

Rayfe laughed. "Well, I think you'd be far more welcome in here than I would be out there."

"Yes, I think you're right. Aren't there things you would like to do but think you can't. As in, this society stops you?"

Rayfe looked down, and Mia followed his gaze to their touching hands.

"Yes, I missed you, I would have liked to be able to contact you, ask how you are, and find out if you were ill. I can phone you in the future but only if you give me your number. I don't even know if you live alone or if my phoning would cause you a problem?"

"I do live alone, and I would love to have phone calls from you."

"Does no sex today mean no kissing either?"

"I hope not." Mia squeezed his hand. "I could be talked into kissing."

&&&

"Matriarchy promises to be no more honest than patriarchy when, in Gramsci's words, "To tell the truth is revolutionary."

Shake society up like a snow globe and white stuff will swirl

But when it settles

The dominant ideas in society

Will be those of the people who are dominant

Using the agencies of their ideological domination

Marx, Gramsci, two men who told us this truth."

Notes for a speech delivered to a secret meeting of anti-government conspirators in the second decade under Matriarchy.

Chapter Ten

Shower

Mia lay on the bed, and her heavy eyelids closed. She forced herself to stay awake, listening, concentrating, thinking. The beds at West Beach were wonderfully comfortable. Amazing, in that they were not there for all night sleeping, and they must surely see a lot of action. Right then, despite waiting for a man to ravish her, she could have happily drifted off.

Total exhaustion due to work meant Mia didn't make the sort of effort that she had been making when she was visiting Rayfe regularly. She simply didn't have the time to sort out sexy clothes and today she had come straight from the lab in a lightweight brown dress suit and sensible flat shoes. She had not been doing lab-based research but had spent the day pouring over data in old, already published, research papers and had still not shared her concerns with any colleagues.

She wonder if he'd notice the lack of effort or if he'd just assume this was another side to Mia. She lay there, feeling too tired to attend to the unbrushed hair or crumpled linen clothes.

A tap on the door forced her eyes open.

"Come in," Mia called, and she was glad she was awake to see this.

Wearing a black suit and white shirt with the top two buttons undone Rayfe sauntered into the room looking as sexy as ever. He didn't rush, he was in no hurry. He had the cool mien of someone who knew he looked good and who knew Mia enjoyed looking at him. He walked to the end of the bed and posed.

"You look too good for what I've got in mind," Mia said, the sight of him energized her, suddenly she was fully awake and glad to be alive.

"What would that be?" he asked.

"I've come straight from work with no chance to shower, I thought you might join me, but it's a shame to get your clothes off."

"I'll put them back on later," he smiled.

"Come on then."

Mia got up and turned her back on him, "Can you undo me."

"I'm sure I will undo you."

Big smiles spread across their faces.

She felt his hand on her waist while the other pulled down the zipper that ran the length of the back of her dress. He eased the straps of the dress over her shoulders so that it fell to the floor. Before she could consider moving, he was at her bra clip and it was undone. She walked away from the pile of clothes towards the shower room wearing only her knickers.

Mia turned on the water and stepped into the spray without waiting for Rayfe. They had showered together before but always after having sex. It was certainly good to turn things around. She turned to see Rayfe ready to join her in the shower. Standing close up to her and completely naked it always amazed her just how big he was. Tall, broad, with a hairy chest and dark trail running down to the treasure. She looked down and was almost surprised to see that he was not erect. Why should he be? He cannot walk around like that all night and have a hard-on at all times in Mia's company. After all, her pussy was not swollen and wet with excitement, not yet.

He joined her under the warm water.

Unsurprisingly the showers are all big enough for two. In fact, they'd probably be a perfect fit for four and Mia was certainly aware that there could be a need for that, even though she had not been tempted to try a threesome or more some.

"Do you ever get involved in threesomes?" How had that slipped out? Was Mia losing the ability to keep some thoughts in her head?

Rayfe didn't look at all surprised as if someone asked him this every day. "Is that something that interests you?"

"No I don't think so but I asked you first."

"Yes, I've been in threesomes. It's just a part of the job."

Like seeing me when I call is just a part of the job.

Mia turned around, how foolish she had been to bring it up. Now she imagined him with other women, and that's not how she liked to think of him.

With her back towards him, she pushed herself gently against his large frame. Her head slotted snugly beneath his chin, and she felt the heat from his hot body against hers. She felt his cock against the small of her back, not hard, but not soft either. Perhaps, actually, he did seem to have a semi-erection most of the time he was with her.

She reached for the soap; she wanted to feel clean before she got dirty. Rayfe's longer arms meant he could reach further than she could and her got to the soap first. With his hands lathered up he worked the suds down her back with the most wonderful massaging movements. It reminded her of the first time they had met.

"I am clean, I've just showered before getting here," he whispered through the spray, his mouth gently touching her ear sending sparks of excitement shooting down her neck. He continued moving his hands over her skin using soapy water to lubricate his movements.

Whether it was the warm water, the soapy massage, or the naked skin against skin she could feel Rayfe's cock swelling and felt herself increasingly enjoying the touches, not just of his magical talents hand but his firm, muscular body against hers.

Having soaped herself all over, she felt she was ready to face him, all the stress of recent weeks washed away by the combination of powerful water jets and soap.

She turned to face him, with her head tilted up, his mouth quickly found hers, and at last they locked in a passionate embrace. His arms wrapped around her body and he held her so close, felt she must be special to someone who holds her this way.

For an age, they stood wrapped in this wet and warm hold, tongues exploring mouths. He tasted so good even better than she remembered and even through the water she could detect his distinctive scent of clean. Lost in the moment, Mia became aware that his big strong body had slowly, carefully but deliberately pinned her to the shower wall. She was unable to move as he held her in place against the cold tiles, she gasped when his wandering hands reached the warm wet place between her legs and his fingers expertly touched her there.

Mia allowed herself to be taken in hand in every way by the man of her fantasies. Rayfe was looking after her, in every sense of the word, was just what she needed. She had proven herself a strong, sexy seductress in their previous encounters; she didn't need to be in control every time. Letting Rayfe take the lead was wonderfully liberating. Giving up control and trusting in a man's judgment took more self-confidence than Mia had in her earlier visits to the unit. In fact, only after many sessions with Rayfe did she feel ready to trust him like this.

***

He found her utterly irresistible and when she turned to him in the shower, he lost a little self-control, lost his cool, completely. He held her close, and she felt so tiny and delicate in his arms, but he knew she was far from fragile. He kissed her not just with passion or desire but with meaning, he hoped his body could communicate to her that he was attracted to her, he needed her like he needed no other woman. This wasn't because she paid him to be there, this was because he wanted to be there.

Even though she had been in control of their earlier encounters today she was different, she was putting up no resistance. Her body language was speaking loud and clear, saying, come and take me. He wanted her, and he needed to touch her, he wanted to please her as much as she pleased him. To feel her wetness, he wanted to make her weak at the knees, he wanted her to beg him for more.

After bringing her to a knee-trembling orgasm as she stood in the shower, he lifted her out and wrapped her in a large, fluffy, white towel. Without drying themselves, he carried her to the bed placed her on it and lay down next to her cradling her in his arms. As this was such a hot summer's night, there was no chance of them getting cold. They resumed the deep kissing, started in the shower, his hard cock pressing into her.

"I want you more than you can know," he said *and I think I'm falling in love with you, but I'm not ready to say that out loud*. Rayfe was losing his mind with desire. The urge to tell her how he really felt conflicted with the training and a decade of being professional, not saying the wrong thing went along with the job of providing sex for payment.

"I want you too." She looked content, but lust burned in her eyes.

"I don't mean just like this," he said. "I want the real you, all of you, I want to really know you." Rayfe reached out to pick up the condom that he had taken out of the packet and put within handy reach when Mia disappeared into the shower.

She simply moaned he felt good, and they were both so aroused that sensible conversation was out of the question.

He got on top, slipped inside and fucked until she was writhing and moaning with a pleasure that seemed to be sexier and more intense than any previous encounter. That could just be because it was happening right now and not a memory of the best sex he had ever had, which also happened to be with her.

She came and, inevitably, the clamping of her muscles around his cock sent him over the edge too.

Even after the frantic thrusting stopped, the kissing didn't. They kissed until Rayfe thought they were at serious risk of red raw faces that may still be evident the next day. He pulled away from her, and she smiled one of those blissful post-orgasmic, satisfied smiles.

At what point in a session with a client do you risk telling them exactly how you feel? He'd never done it before. This one thought was going round in Rayfe's head. Take the chance, she may feel the same, you think the feeling is mutual. How could he say it? What exactly was he to say and why, what would it change anyway? He wanted her. He wanted to fuck her every day. He was overwhelmed with a longing to be with her, to run away with her.

Run away? Was that an option?

"Mia, if you could change things, what would you change?"

"Easy, I'd be doing this every day," she replied. "What about you?"

"Me too, every day with you," he said, he needed to say more. "I can't stop thinking about you, you know."

"Things could change. From the work I've been doing I think there is a very real possibility that we could raise the ratio of male to female births and look towards equality of the sexes."

Was she talking about her work now? Really? That was it. Well fucked and then switch off, back on to the science work that kept her away for three weeks.

"Tell me?" He wasn't interested. He felt a little angry that she'd switched her focus back on to work instead of on them.

"Well, reproduction isn't normally my field I've just been focusing on it around the clock for this particular project that I told you about yesterday. You know that's why I couldn't get here for a few weeks."

"Yes, you explained that." There was a coolness to his tone but she didn't seem to notice it.

"And it's why I look exhausted."

"You look beautiful." He meant it.

"Thank you, but I hope I don't normally look so tired. I've been investigating the repopulating problem and I think I've spotted solutions that are obvious and simple they just need government support to be implemented. We could have as many boys being born as girls."

"Are you saying that years from now there could be as many teenage boys as there are girls and it's all down to you?" *That is certainly impressive but it makes no difference to us now.* "What an achievement."

"I hope so, but it isn't all down to me," Mia said modestly.

"If they don't need you for the whole time that they are repopulating I would like to have you all to myself."

"Just you and me?" she looked surprised

"Most definitely yes."

Mia sat up to get a good look at Rayfe. "Are you serious or is this just the spiel you give to all the women?"

"You are different Mia, and you must know how

I feel about you," Rayfe replied earnestly. "Sessions aren't like this with anyone else. There is a connection between us. I've never experienced before. You know, you've seen other men. Have those times been like this?"

"No, not at all," Mia confessed.

"You are special to me. You've walked in and changed my life. I'm falling in love with you, and I honestly don't know what to do about it." *On my running shoes, I'm losing control but I didn't mean to tell you that.* He sat in silence for what seemed an age as she looked at him. He'd overstepped the mark.

Mia looked at him, without speaking, for what seemed like just too long, before saying, "I feel the same too."

"This hasn't happened to me before." It was a feeble reply, but Rayfe didn't feel as in control of the situation as he'd like to be.

"Me neither Rayfe, let's just enjoy it and see what happens."

Disappointed, Rayfe couldn't help but read many messages into this reply. It could mean, enjoy it while it lasts. It could mean, she's enjoying it, but other things are more important in her life, such as her career. She seemed very excited about her project and it has obviously been a bigger priority than seeing him lately. All he could do was be himself and hopefully win her over, but over to what? They could never be together in any permanent full-time way, but this was not a thought to dwell on.

"I need another shower," said Rayfe. "Do you want to join me?"

"Well look where that ended up last time," replied Mia with a smile. "Yes, of course I'll join you."

&&&

*"Boys are special because there are so few.
And that is why they must be kept safe.
Some boys and men travel to other Men's Units but the journey is long and treacherous.
The guards of matriarchy will ensure safety for everyone, boys and girls, men and women...
There is a dangerous minority of women who live outside the law and do not abide by our rules...*

*extract from Her-Story,
text book for school girls latest edition.*

Chapter Eleven

The Governor

Mia and Rayfe left the room and walked the length of the corridor hand in hand. It felt good to be together. They kissed goodbye as they reached the exit, and she reluctantly passed through the doors that took her away from him and into the reception hall. It was empty due to the late hour. Few if any women would be arriving later this night, the human traffic through the entrance hall would be on the way out.

The sole receptionist was focused on something behind the desk and didn't look up. Trained in discretion, the receptionists only seemed to see the women who approached them. The two security guards were sitting by the exit doors, they usually appeared to pay little attention to anyone but tonight they both looked up and stared at Mia, making her feel most self-conscious. She hurried towards the door trying to avoid eye contact, as all women did in that room, but intent on confrontation one of the guards stood up directly in Mia's path.

"If you have time Dr Setchell, the governor of

the unit, would like to see you."

"Now?" Caught by surprise Mia knew she had no choice.

***

"Good evening Dr Silwood. Come and take a seat."

Dr Setchell was sitting behind a large wooden desk. Bookcases lined the office walls, and shelves crammed with books and papers were the only decoration. At one end of the room, there were easy chairs arranged around a low coffee table in front of a large fireplace. There was, however, nothing personal in the chamber. It was like a library or a space used for hot desking rather than the personal, private office of the woman in charge. Mia noted the stark contrast to most of the offices at Exlabs, where she worked.

Eight photographs were lying on the otherwise empty desk.

"We have been compromised; have a look at these photos."

Mia picked them up and looked at each one, it took a closer inspection to see they were all images of her entering or leaving West Beach.

"My line of work brings me here to visit the science wing, so these don't prove anything. Where did you get them?"

"The note accompanying these photos says there's more but if you think about it, these alone seem pretty compromising. You have visited the science wing only two or three times." Dr Setchell paused as if this was a question requiring an answer, but Mia saw no reason to confirm any details about her itinerary. The older woman seemed to know too much already.

"And only in the past few weeks, in the height of summer. These photos clearly stretch over a period of time you are have different hair lengths, some are in the winter and it would appear to be cold and dark, probably night-time."

"What do they want? Money?" Mia's pulse was racing, her mind working hard to figure out a safe solution without wanting to show her concern and fear.

"We have no details, as yet, whoever took these is just letting us know they have them."

"It isn't illegal to visit the men here."

"It is not, but most women prefer discretion. Take yourself, for example, what would your colleagues think, or your employer? They might feel that your judgment can't be trusted, question your ability to do your job because of your unusual proclivities."

Mia sat silently running things over in her head. Dr Setchell also sat calmly in silence. She was an older woman, probably nearing retirement, and her demeanor projected a self-confidence that came from authority.

"Dr Setchell, doctor of what?" Mia deflected attention from herself for a moment but was genuinely interested in the person who ran this unit.

"Psychology, and you?"

"Biochemistry. What can I do about the photos?"

"I can't say at the moment but I have worked here for almost forty years. There have been many challenges, as you can imagine, but so far, we have always found ways to overcome them. We have to, our success depends on it."

"Are there more photos?"

"These are all we have here, but quite possibly. You know the building has windows. We are remote but a person committed to capturing shots with the right equipment just might be lucky. You had lunch with a man the other day. I expect you ate by the window?"

"I could have been interviewing him, gathering background information for my research."

"If there was no physical contact, that might be plausible, it would depend on what the photos could show. You might have nothing to worry about if you didn't touch him, at all. Infiltration is unlikely, but we should consider it. If whoever sent these photos also has access to our records that could provide them another layer of damning evidence against you. I don't want to worry you; infiltration is unlikely."

"What information could be gained from your records? I thought the information was secure and confidential."

"We are very careful. The top layer of records that most staff can access doesn't link your real identity to your member number. Only very few of us have access to that level of detail, and it isn't available to computer hackers. Someone intent on breaking the code would have to resort to safe-cracking and working through old-fashioned paper files. If you booked lunch not as the scientist, however, but using your membership number, that could identify you as one of our frequent visitors even though it doesn't reveal your identity. A photograph would do that."

"I see," said Mia. "But you are saying it is unlikely they have your records."

"I don't think so but who knows what lengths the political extremists may go to. They want to close West Beach one way or another. I don't wish to be out of my job any more than you want to out of yours."

"Do you think political extremists are behind these?" Mia pointed to the photos. "What lengths do you think they might go to?"

"I don't know." Dr Silwood, leaned forward placing her hands on the desk as if she were coming to the very crux of the matter. "If this unit closed what would happen to the men who live here? Could you imagine men integrated within The Capital, ever? When that would be at a rate of one man per thousand women? Or do you think that would be a death sentence?"

"I don't think they'd be safe," Mia agreed with a very uneasy feeling about where the conversation was going, or where it had come from.

"Androphobia is the fear of men, and Matriarchy has fueled it. While there is a well-stocked sperm bank, I wouldn't want to be a man outside these walls. Let me ask you a question, doctor, could you sentence the unit to closure with uncertainty for the men who live here. The only possible safety would be far away at the other men's units, some are on isolated islands, you know."

"No, I wouldn't want to do that to the men who live here." Mia wanted to say that these sorts of decisions weren't hers to make and that she had no influence over them, but she felt most uneasy about the conversation and the way she was being led into some sort of collusion with this woman.

"I wonder what would happen to women like you if you couldn't visit men here. There is treatment, of course, you know that."

Women like you, not women like us. Dr Setchell's words echoed in Mia's mind, she isn't like the clients of the unit.

"I'm not sick, and you must know that." Despite feeling vulnerable, the suggestion of deviancy angered Mia. Most of the time she bit back her gut instinct to challenge prejudice but saw no reason to let this go unchallenged here.

"It doesn't matter whether I think you are sick or not, the abrupt end of my career here also means the end of access to men for people like you. We're both intelligent women and I'm asking you to support the men living here by supporting the continued existence of the unit. Not for me. Firstly, for the men and, secondly, for women like you." For a woman in her senior years Dr Setchell was intimidating, it wasn't just the way she spoke but the way her eyes didn't leave Mia's face, as if searching for signs of agreement, dissent or weakness.

"I would, but I don't see how."

"Maybe there isn't anything you can do but it would be good to know you are on our side if need be. I can make things a lot easier for you. If you would like to visit more frequently, spend the night or come and go anytime. Anything is possible for our valued clients and for couples who are in love."

In love! How does Setchell know this stuff? Rayfe had used that word today in the room, but it was the only time either of them had said it, how could she know? An uneasy feeling of panic coupled with nausea started to take hold inside Mia, she desperately wanted to get away from that building.

How private was that conversation with her lover? She remained silent and forced her features to stay impassive to Setchell's provocations.

"You think about it, and I'll see what I can do about the pictures. So long as my position is secure here, I will be in the right position to help you. If closure of the unit is pending, I might not be able to protect you."

***

Sleep eluded Mia that night as she reworked Setchell's words in her mind. The thinly veiled threats weren't explicit and yet the implication was unavoidable. The protection of Mia's confidentiality wouldn't be possible if the future of West Beach were under threat. Indeed, if it were Mia herself who threatened that future, then exposing her and discrediting her could only be to Setchell's advantage.

It wasn't illegal to visit men at West Beach and it wasn't a crime to feel as she did, to want to have sex with men. Exposure as a deviant, however, certainly wouldn't bode well for her career. There was no protection for the deviant minority, no anti-discrimination legislation.

Her exposure would probably attract front-page tabloid coverage due to her job preparing the paper for the government's summit and consequently bring into question whatever she put in the report and discrediting Exlabs purely by association. If her work supported the entrenchment of practice at West

Beach, then she could count on Dr Setchell's support. If her proposals threatened the future of the unit, then she could kiss goodbye to her career and her evidence would be dismissed anyway.

Speculating on a conspiracy theory and digging up evidence to support it could only be a losing path for Mia's future. There was only one winning path to choose.

Maybe supporting Setchell would be a good move. If Rayfe was right, the men liked living there and didn't want change. As people, they should have a voice in what happens to them and the future of humanity but no one was consulting this minority and they had no advocate.

The Governor offered greater access to Rayfe as a bribe. Dr Setchell had implied some couples formed long lasting bonds, akin to marriages of olden times, in her news interview many months previously. It wasn't clear how that would work but it was something that certainly stirred Mia's interest. Would Rayfe like that, she wondered, and how could such things be possible within the current Matriarchal system? But why would Dr Setchell want her as an ally?

The fact that Dr Setchell wanted to see her after she had discussed her research, in private, with Rayfe didn't escape Mia's concern. Was it really in private or was that conversation being listened to? There was no other way for anyone to know about Mia's thoughts, she hadn't even discussed them with her work colleagues and it would explain why Setchell hinted that Mia and Rayfe were in love after what he said.

Conversely, perhaps there was no need to look for a conspiracy theory. Mia's preparation for the summit wasn't a secret, and perhaps West Beach were seeking all the allies it could find. As for being in love, Rayfe had used these words and Mia wasn't sure what to say in return but she had been visiting Rayfe frequently and exclusively, that might suggest something to Setchell. Rayfe told her he loved her, perhaps he has discussed his feelings with others inside West Beach. They employ psychologists; even Dr Setchell is a psychologist. Of course, Rayfe could be discussing his feelings even though Mia had no one to confide in.

I don't need to make hasty decisions I need to look at the data again.

Unable to change the situation with the photographs Mia decided to focus on her work.

***

Your brain can perform strange and amazing feats when you aren't aware of it. If you go to bed with a problem, you can wake up with a solution without seeming to do a whole lot of thinking. Yet, if you had stayed up all night instead working on the problem, would you arrive at the same solution? No, you would just be tired.

As a hard working scientist, Mia knew how it felt to burn the midnight oil, working most of the night but the next morning she awoke with a revelation. She had collapsed into her bed fully clothed, woke up after a few hours feeling uncomfortable and removed some. Fortunately, she didn't become fully roused but drifted into a meditative state between consciousness and sleep, when she awoke before her alarm and lay in her bed waiting for the shrill sound to summon her, a new way to look at the problem started to emerge.

It involved politics, of course, it was really a political problem and she wasn't a politician. She was not, therefore, sure how to take her idea forward but perhaps she should clarify it a little. It was time to bounce ideas off someone entirely independent but first there was yet more tests to run in the lab.

"Dr Silwood, there was someone from West Beach to see you here this morning. I left a note on your desk." The lab technician stopped Mia on the stairwell as Mia climbed the flights up to her department.

"Thank you."

"I thought it was strange that she was here so early just hoping to see you without an appointment. I know you're often the first in but it was very early."

"OK." Mia was about to continue.

"Whoever let her in should have dealt with her; I just found her wandering around our lab when I arrived."

"What time was it?"

"Before seven."

"That is early for a visitor, but I know they start early too and I guess she was trying to be super-efficient by coming here before going to work." Mia didn't believe the explanation as she said it, but no need to alert her junior colleague to her discomfort at this information. A feeling of doom took hold of her as she mounted the remaining steps.

Before entering her office, Mia went to check on her work. It came as no surprise, the samples from West Beach had been clearly labeled and were now all missing. She went to the cupboard and was relieved to see all of her notebooks were exactly as she left them, notebooks containing handwritten results of her tests. She still had the data, but no hard evidence and it might not be possible for anyone to replicate her results.

It was time to get an outsider's point of view.

&&&

"The world population exceeded seven billion at the time of the pandemic.

The number of survivors was tiny in comparison.

Even though the vast resources of the world are still available to us,

we no longer have enough people with the skill and knowledge

to live in the same way

as the previous generation."

extract from Her-Story,
text book for school girls
published when Mia's grandmother was a child.

Chapter Twelve

The Bar

Mia walked through the propped open door to the bar at a little after two in the afternoon. The aroma of food with undertones of sweat and beer greeted her. The bar was cavernous and almost empty now, but the mess across the floor and tables covered with dirty plates and glasses confirmed that it had been a busy lunchtime.

"Minetta!" The woman dressed all in black, complete with black apron, put down the pile of plates she was carrying and turned to her colleague. "Carry on. You know what to do."

"Stella, so glad you could see me but are you too busy?" Mia asked.

"Not at all. I know it looks bad but the team will be on top of this chaos quickly, we are used to it you know. This happens every lunch time, and you should see it after closing time." She was removing her apron as she spoke. "Come and sit, I've cleared a few tables already."

Mia followed her sister around to a different section of the L-shaped room and was relieved to see that it clear of used plates and glasses and the floor looked clean too. The carnage of the other section could almost be ignored.

"Business is going well then? You appear to be busy."

"Yes. Very well and too busy! Take a seat I'll just go get rid of this," she held up the apron.

Mia didn't feel guilty about leaving work shortly after midday and made no excuses about going to visit her sister at a bar on the other side of town. She told her colleagues she was going to work from home because she had left so many old reports piled up high in her apartment, with pages open for cross-referencing. It was true and it wasn't practical to pick them all up and bring them to her office in the daytime. No one doubted that Mia had been working excessive hours at home ever since being told about the summit. Although, in reality they all knew that is how Mia worked on most things, flat out and thorough, few others could keep up with her pace.

Within minutes, Stella was back holding a bottle of red wine in one hand and two glasses in the other. Stella was a few years older and couldn't have been more different, she had no interest in science. She was gregarious, the perfect personality for running a bar and nightclub, as she did.

"Is this okay for you?"

"I'm sure it will be. Thanks."

Stella slid into the booth, and a waitress came over with a large tray of mezze.

"We shouldn't drink on empty stomachs, so tuck in, there's plenty," Stella said.

"You're drinking in the middle of the

afternoon?" Mia was surprised as she assumed her sister might have to work that night.

"As soon as you called I got someone to cover me later. I can do that being the boss," she smiled. "But we might as well stay here in my bar, where the food is good and the wine is free. At least for now, while it is quiet, anyway."

"Well, thanks. I didn't expect you to feed me."

"It isn't every day you come over, it's barely once a year, and you look like you could do with feeding!" Stella poured the wine. She was as slim as her sister was, even if she did eat and drink more, running around for her business apparently burned the calories.

"Well, I appreciate it. You know I don't get out much." Mia realized she had been surviving on biscuits, so she tucked into bread and hummus to give the red wine a soft landing.

"You sounded like you need to talk. What's on your mind?"

"Is it that obvious?" Mia's free hand curled around the stem of the wine glass as she picked at the food.

"Yes. I can't think why you'd want talk to me, though, if it is about science or your job, they're the only things important to you, and I know nothing about them."

"You live in the same world I do so you can give me valuable insights on many things,"

"I'm intrigued, do go on." Stella leaned forward, encouragingly.

"It's politics, you work in a bar, meet lots of different people I read the papers and watch the news but I'm wondering what other people think about the population issue and the men."

"You can't believe everything you read in the press, sis." Stella was smiling and didn't seem to think this was a serious subject.

"Those aren't burning issues on the lips of every customer. People talk about their day at work, their annoying neighbors, their annoying bosses, their annoying work colleagues and how expensive everything is. They discuss how things are unreliable and are so often breaking down. They don't talk about population growth or men. I'd say the things that concern most women are the things that directly affect them personally on a daily basis."

"Oh, that's interesting. Completely different to what I expected."

"Why's that? Do the women in science behave differently?"

"You know we're located near West Beach."

"I do indeed." Stella raised her eyebrows and lowered her tone in a somewhat knowing way. She tore at some flat bread and dipped it in hummus.

"Some of our work can involve men or reproduction in some way. So it does come up in regular conversation."

"Now I am interested."

"Not in a hands-on way. No, we might have data from past research, ancient research, but it was often only done on men, and we can't be sure that the results would replicate with women. That sort of thing is a daily issue. Some of the problems we are investigating and trying to solve may be down to the pre-Matriarchy pandemic."

"You mean the plague, I always love the way you talk, it's not like the rest of us!" Stella teased.

"I've told you before it wasn't a plague, but we don't need to get into that, you're only trying to wind me up."

"That's right!" Stella scoffed with a cheeky grin. "Let's save the fun stuff for when we're on to bottle number three."

"Winding up the geek girl is a strange idea of fun. Seriously, can I tell you about my current project? It may sound really boring, but you must not breathe a word to anyone."

"Sure, no problem. Who would I discuss your science project with anyway?" Stella replied while topping up their glasses, which seemed to have miraculously emptied themselves.

"Well, it might sound like no big deal so it's the sort of conversation you might have casually with a stranger, but it could be an enormous deal. There's going to be an emergency government summit in few weeks' time and I am preparing one of the papers. It's looking at the population problem. Firstly, they need to work out if there is a problem. Is the population stable, declining or growing and do we have enough fertile people to make future generations. Secondly, would it be second? I'm already rambling, that wine is having an effect. Next! Next, we need to know if there is a cure for the widespread infertility."

Stella was nodding and looking interested. Mia hungrily eyed the barely eaten food but with her sisters full attention she continued, she could eat later.

"Then it would be over to the politicians to decide what to do with our recommendations but politicians are swayed by the electorate, women like you and your customers. Our lab, scientists in general, are concerned with that second issue, curing infertility. Can we treat or cure infertility, is there any way to produce more fertile men as their numbers are so low."

"So you might have a cure? That would be fantastic, you will be so famous!" Stella looked pleased as if sitting with a future celebrity.

"I'm not sure about a cure, but I may have a solution to increase the number of male births, but even then I'm not sure whether they would be fertile or not." Mia wasn't hoping for fame and attention.

"I see, but do we want more men?" Stella looked as if she were giving the matter some thought.

"Yes, that is the question."

"I think the answer would be a resounding no. Keep things as they are or have less of them, men that is. No one says we should have more and everyone knows there are sperm banks and alternative techniques. If anyone ever brings up the subject, you will find overwhelming support for producing babies just from women without any male DNA involved, that's a popular idea."

"But that is a dangerous unproven path to go down."

"I know, we are all aware. Someone always raises those objections. I'm just telling you it is popular."

"Are you saying that no one wants normal fertility restored and as many boys being born as girls?" Mia already knew the answer to this question, before visiting Stella, but she had to get it confirmed because she often had difficulty believing her own views were so far out of step with the popular majority.

"Oh heavens! I think people would consider that to be a national disaster. No political party would be elected with that in their manifesto, and if by some miracle it happened overnight I really don't know what would happen." Stella leaned forwards and whispered. "I think I need more wine before talking about such a thing, even contemplating it. A lot more wine."

The women both picked up nuts and sat silently reflecting for a while.

"Have you been to West Beach?" Stella glanced at Mia, eyes meeting for a second before she returned to choosing her next stuffed mushroom, giving the matter more attention than it needed.

"For my work," Mia replied shuffling uncomfortably in her seat and hoping the flushed feeling wasn't showing in her face.

"Yes for your work, of course," Stella said looking up.

"Yes. I've been there," Mia's whisper was barely audible, but Stella cold probably read her lips.

"I've been there too."

For a moment Mia was confused, why would Stella go to that place then slowly the only possible reason dawned on her.

"Oh."

"I've never told anyone but I thought you might understand," Stella looked down again, unable to meet her sister's gaze.

"I do understand. We're sisters, we're the same." Mia wasn't sure what to say, this wasn't what she was expecting although there was a certain feeling of relief in having shared her secret with someone.

"Let's take this conversation somewhere more private."

"Yes, let's." Mia agreed.

"I've got more wine in my flat upstairs, but we can carry the food up. It's handy living above the bar." Stella was on her feet in an instant as if to run away and leave behind the cat that was let out of the bag at their table.

The door to Stella's apartment was behind the bar, Mia followed her older sister, both of them bearing bowls of food. On the way, Mia noticed that during the time they were talking the staff had restored order and cleanliness to the rest of the venue.

When seated with fresh drinks from what was only their second bottle Stella asked, "Did you mean what I thought you meant when you said we're the same?"

"Perhaps it's in our genes?"

"Drop the science talk, sister. You've been to see the men too?" Stella demanded a straight answer.

"I didn't expect to be talking about it but yes. I have been seeing one man in particular. No one else knows, except the staff there."

"Well of course the staff know, you mean the guards, don't you. It's a funny thing to say. As I always say, you don't talk like the rest of us."

Not when you've had chats in the governor's office, and she knows you better than your own sister, thought Mia, but she replied, "Yes, I mean the guards. I don't know if it's a funny thing to say, as I've never talked about it. Have you?"

"Well, I probably move in very different circles to you, given our work. There is a sort of underground network of women who are a bit different, not mainstream. They meet at clubs and bars."

"Here?" Mia asked with surprise.

"No, not at mine. This place is very mainstream."

"Before we talk about that, and I would like to,

and before I have more to drink..." Mia wanted to focus on the primary purpose of her visit before being distracted by alcohol and tangents.

"So while you still know what we're saying," Stella interrupted.

"Exactly. I want to ask your opinion. It might be possible to repopulate, in that, there are as many male births as female births and we even up the male to female ratio. All my life I thought that was the goal. To get things back to how they were before the pandemic. Reverse the effects of the virus. But, I am thinking, just because we can do that it doesn't mean we have to. If we can control the male birth rate perhaps central government might determine that it stays at its current level. It stays low and the men continue to live separately. What do you think of that."

"You are waffling on, almost incoherently, but, I think you just might be on the same page as the rest of us, at long last."

"Do you mean, you personally would like things to stay as they are, even though you like men."

"I like to visit men there, occasionally. Apart from that I'm like all the other bigoted women, I am afraid of what increased male numbers would mean for us all."

"You know they're not the monsters that we are taught to think they are."

"The ones I've met are fine at West Beach, but I don't know if they are all like that. Who's to say they'd be the same if they were in greater numbers or if they lived among us. Maybe those we've met are the only civilized ones."

"How can you say that?" Stella's views surprised Mia, but that is why she went there, for frank talking.

"Can you really say that you find it acceptable, the thought of men and women living together?" Stella replied defiantly.

"Well we have done throughout most of history," Mia's backed up her answer with scientific fact, as was so often the case.

"And what a sorry story that has mostly been," Stella's reply was based on modern history and her story lessons.

"Can I get a glass of water?" Mia stood up and was on her way to the kitchen without waiting for a reply. The effect of the wine was helping to loosen their tongues but she didn't want to lose track of the conversation altogether, which would defeat the purpose of her visit in the first place, to clarify things. She found two large glasses and filled them with water.

"If you want my opinion on what women want, most women," Stella said as Mia sat down. "I think they want the population to increase because we are told it is worryingly low, but how would we know that? And, they don't want things to be as they were before Matriarchy, not in any way, so not more men just more women."

"I expect you're right," Mia agreed.

"Do you remember that case of lawyer and the man who lived together? It came out about two years ago?" Stella asked, leaning forward to pick up the second glass of water.

"Yes, vaguely. Why, did you know them?"

"No but they lived very near here. I could hear the protesters when they were outside their door."

"I remember it in the news, everyone was talking about it. He dressed up as a woman but didn't leave the house except in the dark and in the winter, then he went about well wrapped up and inconspicuous. They didn't have visitors either so they got away with living together for years. But what a life."

"What a life. When they were caught it was such a scandal, even though that man had bothered no one."

"Do you know what happened to them?" Mia asked.

"They disappeared. I don't know, perhaps he went to a Men's Unit. Even though everyone treated her like a criminal she couldn't go to prison she hadn't actually commit a crime. I think people wanted her to be guilty of something."

"So where would she disappear to?"

"Perhaps it was suicide or even murder or maybe they went together. Ran away, to live together in the abandoned towns in the countryside?" Stella speculated.

With the population being only a fraction of what it once was most towns were left abandoned. Ruined ghost towns stood the length and breadth of the country, with buildings, now in a sorry state. Looting, which was described as an organized process of reclaiming, meant there was little of value left inside the decaying houses, shops, offices and warehouses. With many empty buildings property, especially dwellings, ceased to have any value. People could pick and choose where they lived.

"Do you think that's possible? To live somewhere else, outside society I mean."

After the pandemic, most women moved to The Capital, or to towns nearby, to live secure, orderly lives. There was a big expanse of abandoned countryside for those who wanted to live outside the law, outcasts, outsiders and anarchists living by their own rules.

"No, I couldn't imagine doing it, but people do talk about it. There are rumors that men and women live together in far off countries. But they are just rumors. I couldn't imagine you living as a wild fugitive either."

Stella and Mia both laughed at the thought.

"At the moment most people are asexual, and those with no sexual desires are dictating to us all how we should behave."

"You've a good point there, we can agree on that. Even the sex clubs for women are so discrete they're hard to find."

"Sex clubs for women," Mia's eyebrows rose with interest. "Have you been to those too?"

"Sister, where have you been? Oh, I know, nowhere right?" Stella was giggling again.

"Right." Nodding with incredulity Mia replied, "So tell me about these clubs."

"Well, they tend to be in basements or upstairs rooms, difficult to get to, most often involving a trek to some of the poorer parts of suburbia. Dark, too much noise."

"Get to the details, Stella, we've drunk enough to make me slur! Now, details!"

"Women who want to feel sexy go. They don't all do stuff, some just like the hot atmosphere or hope to meet women with similar interests. Some of the women are lesbians, others, I'm not sure. I would say some might be into men and like to act out that fantasy with some of the butch dykes who are packing."

"Packing?"

"Packing, wearing a strap-on dildo packed in their trousers. I'm not saying they're all into men, as some probably just like their lesbian lovers to be like that. A bit of fantasy role play, you know."

"I beg your pardon." Mia was surprised, not shocked.

"You've no right to judge when you've been playing with the real thing. Most women would find that shocking. Anyhow, now you tell me something. Like how often do you go to see men."

"About twice a month."

"Twice a month! That's a lot!" It was Stella's turn to look amazed.

"Why how often have you been?" Mia asked.

"Well, in my whole life, I think I've been less than ten times, ever. How many times for you? When did you start going."

"I started going there about eighteen months ago but I must say for a lot of the time, perhaps most of the time, it has been once a month." Following Stella's comments, Mia was too self-conscious to admit to the fact that her visits had mostly been far more frequent.

"Why sometimes more frequently?"

"Because I met someone special," Mia looked down at the glass in her hands, concerned about how this revelation would be taken. It was one thing to admit seeing men and another to admit to having feelings for one of them, especially after her sister was so hostile towards the idea of equality.

Stella sighed, "Are you in love?"

"Are you going to mock me if I say yes?"

"So you are!" There was the distinct sound of joy in Stella's tone.

"I don't know if I'm in love, but I'm very keen

on him. I can't stop thinking about him when we're apart."

"I think it is sweet. Are you enjoying it or do you want to be healed?"

"Now you're mocking. I'm addicted to him so much that it hurts so, yes, I want to be cured." Mia couldn't believe she was telling her sister this, that's too much wine talking.

"Not really Huh?" Stella joked.

"No, not really."

"Maybe if you broadened your horizons, went to some of these clubs I mentioned, perhaps he'd stop seeming so special."

"I don't think so. It is to do with the whole man. The way he talks, the things he says, his smell and not just how he looks. Women aren't as big and hairy as that even if they have a false dick between their legs." The women giggled.

"All true. For those reasons some women prefer the girls with dicks and actually aren't into men at all. Men love 'em and leave 'em. They're not for relationships they are for sex, that's what I say."

&&&

"The increasingly popular Daughters of Scum are demanding that the government withdraw any financial support from the Men's Units. They say female guards should no longer be posted to them and resources should not be sent.

A spokeswoman said, "Many women are struggling to survive, especially in the winter months.

We should be looking after each other and the men should take care of themselves."

The government have responded, stating that the male units are fully self sufficient and self funding. They do not divert much needed resources from women."

Extract from a contemporary news item.

Chapter Thirteen

A Picnic

Rayfe was stunned when Dr Setchell approached and addressed him personally by name. It was first thing in the morning. Rayfe and his friends were on their way to the office to check out the day's work; something they had taken to doing before breakfast and often before showering or anything else. The men rarely saw the governor, and when they did it was usually at a distance, walking along a corridor or giving a speech on a special occasion. Most have probably not spoken to her, nothing more than a polite acknowledgment.

"Rayfe can I have a word with you, please."

"Yes." Wide-eyed with surprise that the governor singled him out by name, Rayfe stood motionless. He couldn't understand how she could know his name, which gave him cause to wonder if she knew every man's name in West Beach.

"There will be a picnic on the beach in a few days' time just for a very select group of ladies, there will be six couples in all and I would like you to invite Mia. I know you have permission to call her."

"Yes, of course, when is it?"

"All of the details are in the office, and if you call Mia now, you might get her before she sets off for work."

Dr Setchell looked at the men gathered around, and Rayfe followed her gaze. They all seemed to be just as surprised him by the interaction they witnessed.

"Paul, you have been booked for the same event. Your companion will be Kerry, she has already confirmed."

"Thank you," Paul replied. What else could he say?

Returning to Rayfe, Dr Setchell continued. "Mia may be hesitant because she's not been to a social event before, if so do all you can to talk her into coming. I know she would like to spend more time here with you and it would be good for her to see more of what we do, don't you think?"

"Yes, I'm sure I can persuade her," Rayfe replied. He thought Mia would like to spend more time with him and see more of West Beach, but this wasn't a conversation he was prepared to have with Dr Setchell as if she were an old mate. They hadn't previously exchanged any words in the ten years he'd been there. In fact, conversations like this usually took place with his trainer, Dr Walsh.

"Is Walsh in today?" he asked.

"Not yet but she will be in later if you want to make an appointment I'm sure she has time to see you."

He expected this answer. Dr Setchell was doing Walsh's job because, in her absence, they wanted him to phone Mia immediately.

***

The day after visiting her sister Mia awoke with a groggy head to an early morning phone call. This caller wouldn't have left a message, so it was fortunate she answered with closed eyes, despite her pounding head.

The friendly voice of Rayfe on the line replied to Mia's grunt. He invited her to an exclusive soiree on the beach in a few days' time. It would be a small social gathering, a picnic for a total of six couples, six men and six women. Another missed work afternoon but it would be worth it to see Rayfe in a different setting, and it just might help her think through her issues. She agreed to go despite the fact that he threatened her with pepitos.

Apart from an enlightening conversation with her sister, Mia had never knowingly met a woman who visited the men at West Beach. She was quite nervous about it. Rayfe assured her that the other women attending were all long time regulars, and they all expected discretion. She could tell Rayfe was impressed and perhaps a little curious as to how Mia gained such a privileged invite, the women who get to attend such exclusive gatherings were usually regular visitors to West Beach for ten years or more.

Upon arrival, the receptionist directed her through the usual door where Rayfe was waiting. They walked to a new part of the building she hadn't previously visited; she knew she had only seen a fraction of it. This trip promised to be a revelation.

She walked along a corridor, where windows along one side gave a view to the grounds of West Beach. The pool and sports courts were nearby, there were tables and chairs for relaxing around a bar area and further sports facilities, in the distance she spied open fields and small buildings. The vista was buzzing with men, although most were in the shade or relaxing as this was the afternoon at the height of summer, on an exceptionally warm August day.

Having come from work Mia was wearing a pink full-length cotton summer dress, smart but lightweight for the sweltering summer weather. In the room at the end of the corridor, five men and three women were already waiting to go on the excursion.

"Come and meet everyone. Everyone this is Mia." Smiling faces greeted her as Rayfe worked his way around the room. The warmth and friendliness of the welcome reassured Mia that her apprehension at meeting the group of people was groundless, nevertheless the nervousness didn't dissipate quickly.

Rayfe introduced his roommate, Paul, Mia felt a little envious of that position, sharing a room with Rayfe. Two of the women were unknown to Rayfe, Brinda and Ruby introduced themselves. Rayfe offered no explanation as to how he knew Rose and Mia felt a pang of jealousy, which she suppressed. Rod, Eric and Tucker all appeared to be much older than Mia and Rayfe, Nico could have been around their age and Paul was obviously was the youngest person present.

"We're just waiting for two more ladies to join us and then the minibus will take us to the beach," said Rose. "We three ladies have all met before."

"A few too many times," agreed Brinda, with far too much hair in many shades of pink Mia bit back the urge to ask if the candyfloss like locks were real hair. Despite her colorful image, her face was that of a mature woman, and she must have been at least in her forties.

"We come to many of these things here, picnics, parties. It's good to have a new woman along," agreed Ruby, another mature woman Mia realized she was by far the youngest; these women were all old enough to be her mum, or almost.

Chatter continued along the lines of how many times or how many years ago the women had met, completely ignoring the men in the room who stood listening in silence. Rayfe and Mia also remained quiet until a guard escorted the final two women into the room a few minutes later.

Before any further introductions could take place the guard spoke, "If you would make your way to the shuttle bus, I will be driving you to the beach." She led the way through the door. It was rare to hear the voice of one of the guards. In their cream and white uniforms they usually disappeared into the background, always there but almost invisible, discreet, unobtrusive and without personal identity.

True to form the guard walked through the exit door without waiting for any response and without making eye contact with any of the twelve people gathered for the day and all present in turn ignored her. "Kerry." The youngest man stepped forward to greet one of the women with a kiss on the cheek, and he took her hand in his. Mia noticed that this woman looked as nervous as she felt, perhaps another first-timer to this type of event.

At the same time, the three female friends welcomed the other woman, Lorri.

"Kerry, Lorri, Mia, let's continue chatting on the

beach," said Rose following the guard through the door.

"I expect the picnic awaits," Ruby agreed.

"And towels for swimming," added Brinda.

"As if you'd get your hair wet!" Rose poked her friend as they paused by the door to the shuttle bus parked immediately outside.

"I might dip a toe and someone else might swim."

"I enjoyed watching the boys in the water last year. Swimwear not allowed." Coquettish Lorri had just arrived and Mia wasn't sure how she felt about the bunch of women who were all so familiar with each other.

It was just a very short drive to the beach, around the perimeter of the men's unit. The journey took a matter of minutes even in the electric powered shuttle bus, which moved little faster than walking pace.

When they left the vehicle and trailed across the sand, Rayfe and Mia fell towards the back of the crowd, along with Paul and Kerry. The view of the large gazebo offering much-needed shade from the burning sun and the equipment for the gathering couldn't fail to impress the guests. There were sunbeds; a table covered by a spread of food and drinks kept cool with strategically placed blocks of ice, and some curious boxes piled under the table. Two men were sitting in the shade but got up and walked back in the direction of the men's unit as soon as they saw the party crowd.

"What are they doing?" asked Mia.

"Looking after our picnic venue, keeping it safe from the wind and the seagulls," Rayfe replied.

"We blokes all set the stuff up here earlier

today," said Paul. "They just brought the food out at the last minute."

"What's under the table?" she asked Rayfe as they drew near enough for her to see.

"Anything we might need, guitar, towels, beach ball, you see the net is set up ready for beach volleyball."

"Guitar?"

"Sing-a-longs are surprisingly popular, but if you prefer I can serenade you."

"Sounds good."

"Which one?"

"Both. I'd love to hear you play again, of course."

Mia looked past Rayfe, into the eyes she felt burning into her.

"Sorry, I didn't mean to stare, it's just that you look familiar," Kerry smiled.

"I don't think I know you," Mia replied but thought differently, Kerry also looked familiar, but Mia couldn't remember from where.

"Ladies I must join in this conversation. We have adopted an excellent rule of not knowing each other outside of these walls. Well, not that there are walls on the beach but you know what I mean." Rose indicated Lori, Brinda and Ruby. "We all seem friendly with each other but it's only in this context, we don't meet outside, we don't know each other outside of here."

"Rose is right. No matter if you think you know someone here, just put it out of your head. What happens here stays here," Brinda said.

"We don't talk about our real lives or jobs," Ruby agreed. "This is a different life. And it possibly helps to use a pseudonym, with a false identity and wear a massive wig as a disguise, like Brinda." Ruby had a dig at the colorful woman.

"Wig! I'm not going to rise to take the bait!" came Brinda's retort.

After paddling in the shallow seawater to cool down and tucking into the delicious cold buffet the men split into two teams of three to play beach volleyball.

"Only fools go out in the midday sun," Rose had taunted but one of the older men pointed out that the midday sun had passed by more than four hours ago.

The women agreed it was much too hot for beach games, so they settled down in the shade to watch the men. Mia took stock of the group. She and Kerry had the least to say, they hadn't frequented one of these group functions before whereas Rose attended them every week through the summer. The other women were also regular party guests on a long-term basis.

"They have group socials in the winter too, but there are more in the summer," Rose explained. "I try to come along once a week. Make the most of the long day, warm weather and the beach, of course,"

"You make it sound like you aren't here for the men." Lorri didn't take her eyes off the volleyball game. Six fit men jumping about and getting sweaty wearing beach shorts and nothing else did make for an agreeable sight.

"The company is a big bonus," Rose agreed.

Rose was extremely sociable, she acted as the glue to bind the group. Mia couldn't help feeling different, like an outsider. If everyone was part of a couple at this event, whom they were with wasn't obvious. Through conversation, it became clear that, at the very least, Rose and Lorri might be promiscuous predators rather than sticking to one man. Mia hadn't set out looking for love at West Beach either, she hadn't known what she was looking for. She wasn't in a hurry to jump in and judge others in a negative way as she had also met many men, but now she felt different.

Kerry was quiet, apart from commenting on the dangers of sunburn. She obviously came with Paul, which was most surprising as she was in her mid-thirties, almost old enough to be his mother. Admittedly, the other women were older but Kerry seemed so earnest that one couldn't imagine her with a younger friend at all, whereas colorful Brinda looked more like the sort of wild woman who would be interested in a younger man.

***

The boys played volleyball on the fine golden sands under the scorching sun, and the women admired them, but it was too hot for the sport to last for long. Taking a break, the six tore down the beach to take a dip in the cool refreshing water. The women took the cue to join the men, although they stayed at the edge of the shallow water with the waves lapping around toes and ankles or ventured in as far as their knees.

Rayfe spotted Mia and, having cooled down, he swam inland and made his way directly to her. Seeing Mia's partner coming towards them the women moved away, eyes on other men. As he walked out of the water to cover the final short distance between them, the lustful look in Mia's eyes was unmistakable. She liked the look of him naked or in the shower so, of course, she would like the look of him now. Stepping out of the sea his body glistened with moisture. Beads of salt water sat on his shoulders, embedded in the hairs on his chest or trickled a path downwards over his face and arms, where smooth skin assisted the natural force of gravity.

The way she looked at him, with hunger in her eyes, stirred the same desire within him.

"I'm glad you came today, Mia, I miss you."

"Let's get some towels and dry ourselves," she replied.

The happy smile didn't change the noticeable fact of her pale skin and the dark shadows under her eyes. Rayfe cared about this woman, and wanted to help her through whatever was troubling her.

He had missed her when they were apart and when he hadn't seen her for three weeks it had been terrible. Since then, every time he saw her recently she looked increasingly tired, even though she looked good to him he could see she looked troubled. It was as if she had transformed into a different woman, and he cared just as much for this version of Mia, not the woman performing in the bedroom.

"Let's go for a little walk, if we go towards the unit there are sand dunes. Would you like to explore them?" A towel draped over his shoulders, water droplets still glistening on his chest, Rayfe was aware of how he looked and hoped Mia would respond accordingly. The glint in her tired eyes suggested she wanted him as much as ever.

"Yes I enjoy an adventure."

There was still that cheeky twinkle in her eyes.

From April to June he had discovered how adventurous she could be. Adventurous is one word he would use to describe her. If there were more words available, he would say, sexy, seductress, imaginative, serious, intelligent, and different in every way from any women he had previously met, and more.

They climbed to the top of several dunes and down into the dips, where they couldn't see anyone and not be seen. After three or four hillocks, Rayfe pulled Mia close to him and kissed her. Her lips instantly yielded to his demand. The thought of exploring her body replaced any thoughts of exploring the dunes.

He wanted to talk to her, to find out about the problem that has been giving her sleepless nights but the swelling in the front of his trousers demanded a focus on something else, a more urgent, pressing problem.

"I can't hold back you have been turning me on the whole afternoon," he whispered in her ear.

With her body pushing into his and her mouth kissing his Rayfe knew she wanted him too but she pushed him away. A reluctantly insincere gesture with her hands. But Rayfe respected it.

Tears welled in her eyes and Mia cried and cried.

"What's wrong?" he asked enveloping her in his arms.

They huddled together, Mia tucked in close to Rayfe, who folded around her.

"There's so much on my mind I don't know where to start. I'd like to tell you but there is no obvious beginning to the story, and I'm not sure where it ends, either."

"Well you can throw yourself in at the middle and then try to fold up the loose ends later."

"There are lots of threads; if I try to tell you about them, maybe you can tie them up."

"OK."

"There's work. I have to meet my boss in a few days. I should tell her that there seems to be something strange going on here at WB because there is no reason for a low male birth rate. The samples I tested indicated there should be plenty of men."

"Samples?"

"Sperm samples from here and now they're missing."

"There's no shortage if you need more samples!" They smiled together. Rayfe didn't understand the problem, so he encouraged her to continue.

"The evidence was stolen from my lab. I'm certain some of the West Beach team took the samples when they came to visit me."

"Have you confronted them?"

"No."

"Why not?" Rayfe was genuinely confused, struggling to make sense of the conversation. Perhaps this was the reason for the transformation that he had noticed in the woman he loved.

"Because I wish I'd never seen those samples. I don't want to believe they are fixing things here to keep the male numbers exceptionally low. The low rates of fertility among the population wouldn't be such a big problem if at least those who are fertile gave birth to plenty of boys as well as girls."

"Are you saying, a team of women are tampering with the birth rate, and you have no evidence?"

"Not exactly. Yes, I think the WB fertility team are selectively breeding females when they could produce male babies but it doesn't matter that I've lost the evidence. Even without those samples, I have enough past research to point towards a way of raising the rate of male births."

"That's not going to help anyone. I don't think we need more men,"

Mia looked surprised by his answer.

"Not just now," he continued. "To increase the population we don't need more men, we need more fertile women to carry children. Have you thought about looking into that?"

She remained silent.

"You said you have more issues?" he prompted.

"Yes. There's how I feel about visiting here. It has been a great experience."

"Has been great, like, past tense?" What about is still great and will be in the future?

"Yes, past. I don't think I should come here anymore. We live in different worlds, we can't share those worlds, and I find that I spend so much time thinking about you and what might be going on here that it…" She trailed off looking for words, "It isn't healthy. It is distracting, I can't concentrate, and if I'm caught out, identified, my life would be destroyed."

"Is that's it? No discussion? This is the last time?"

Mia didn't reply.

"Do I get a say?" He knew she felt guilty about the imbalance of power that she thought they had. She thought because she could come and go, and she booked and paid for the service the power was disproportionately hers. They'd talked about that, but he knew he had power too. His side of the wall was a better place to live.

"Of course," she said defensively with tears in her eyes. "I want to see you, Rayfe I'm falling in love with you." He wasn't expecting that. "So if you can show me a different and happier way I would be interested."

Rayfe felt like the bottom was dropping out of his world, he wanted to punch something and argue with her that visiting him wasn't wrong. What could he say to convince her when she already admitted she loved him, she had said it. She was in love with him but dumping him and forsaking men forever.

"Can't you compartmentalize. Perhaps make your visits here less often but longer? Or more frequent but shorter? Maybe we could talk by phone more often? You only just gave me your number. I could call you every day. You don't have to choose between me and your life outside," he said, almost pleading. How could he argue against the world outside when he didn't know it?

Tears were freely rolling down her cheeks.

"I don't know," she said. "I need to think."

***

Mia sat in stunned silence for a while. It was a revelation.

Wrapped up in her personal issues, Mia had lost track of the real problem. Again, talking to other people, people who aren't scientists, revealed a solution. Rayfe and her sister, they had both cut to the heart of the problem in a way that she could not.

Why wasn't she as sharp as she used to be?

Perhaps visiting men was too distracting she needed to return to her old self, totally absorbed in science and not distracted by the world around her.

"I love you, Mia." His voice in her ear but almost distant.

&&&

"A number of religious and philosophical organizations have come forward to support the demands of the Daughters of Scum that Matriarchy should severe all connections with the Men's Units.

The key motivation seems to be the government's assertion that the units are self-financing.

There has been no official statement as yet but it seems the disparate groups are united over disapproval of Sex for Sale at the West Beach unit. While some groups disapprove of sex entirely, some disapprove of sex with men and for others the issue is not the physical contact but the exchange of money or the lack of monogamy."

Extract from a contemporary news item.

Chapter Fourteen

A Proposal

"I'm Dr Walsh, Joanne Walsh. It is good to meet you after I've heard so much about you." The stranger held out a hand, which Mia grasped and shook firmly. Dr Walsh had obviously been waiting for Mia, lurking just inside the doors at West Beach.

"I know you've come to see Dr Setchell but I wanted to meet you, so I thought I could accompany you up to her office." She turned to walk alongside Mia.

"What have you heard about me?"

"I'm Rayfe's support worker. I shouldn't really repeat what has said about you but I think you know the sort of thing, all good. That's why I had to meet the superwoman he described."

Mia blushed, feeling flattered, so Rayfe had been confiding in this woman about her.

"I care a lot about Rayfe, I've known him ever since he arrived here ten years ago and I'd hate to see him with a broken heart. May I call you Mia?"

"Yes, Mia's fine." She wondered if he had he told her about them splitting up, about their last conversation when she said she might not visit again?

"What is your role here?" Mia asked.

"I have a team of men that I look after. Whereas Dr Setchell handles everyone and everything, I am just concerned with the well-being of my team. I say team but I know the men as individuals. For the first month or two I see them almost daily for one to one teaching sessions and then I maintain regular contact over the years. I am their confidante for all matters to do with their work and their relationships."

"That must be interesting. When did you last speak to Rayfe?"

"It was a few days ago, could have been last week actually, you know how time flies. Sometimes I might not see some of the men in my team from one month to the next but they will ask to see me if they need me. And Rayfe has wanted to meet with me lately to talk about you. He's smitten, you know that, and sometimes it's good just to have someone independent to talk to about these things. Not the people who are around you every day."

"So what could you tell him? What are the prospects for a man and a woman in love but living here and now?"

"My conversations with him are confidential."

"Ah yes, of course."

"But I could tell him as I can tell you. When two people are in love, we can make arrangements for them at West Beach. Some women come here only looking for sex but you are an educated woman, you know men and women used to live together. We can arrange for you to be together now, even under

Matriarchy, discretely, of course."

"I see," she said, although she did not, she couldn't understand how that could work, "I'd be interested in that."

"Well, why don't we try and make it happen if you and Rayfe are both agreeable and I think he will be most eager."

"It is a bit soon to be planning marriage and our whole lives together." Mia joked and they laughed together.

"Yes sorry, I'm getting carried away. I didn't mean to suggest you rush things but it is so good to see a couple getting along as well as you both seem to. And Rayfe is such a lovely man, sweet and caring."

"You don't need to talk me into liking him," Mia was nodding and smiling in agreement.

"I wasn't trying to. I mean because he is such a lovely person he deserves to have a woman who loves him as much as I know he would cherish her."

If Walsh was push all the right buttons for Mia, the conversation strengthen her resolve to discuss with Dr Setchell how and why she could do the right thing.

Covering up a fraud wasn't right but security for the future of humanity was her priority.

They arrived at the familiar door to Dr Setchell's office.

"I understand you and Dr Setchell have things to talk about but if you'd like to meet with me afterward, I will be just along the corridor there. And if you ever want to speak to me by phone or to meet then just ask for me here. I'm almost always here."

Dr Walsh knocked on Dr Setchell's door.

Dr Setchell opened it in person, welcoming Mia

in with a warm smile and gestured towards an easy chair by the unlit fireplace. Then she sat in a chair facing Mia but away from the formidable desk.

"How have you been? I hope not too distressed by the photos I showed you?"

"No. I've not thought about them much."

Dr Setchell looked surprised.

"You said you could take care of that problem and I've trusted that you can. Hopefully they will never come to light."

"I will do what is within my power," Dr Setchell nodded in a reassuring way. The words were carefully chosen to say that if she were no longer the governor of West Beach then protecting Mia would not be within her gift.

"I've not given the photographs any thought at all because I've had more important things to think about and that's what I was hoping to talk to you about."

Dr Setchell looked unprepared and curious. Mia was delighted by the way her words and her tone of voice gave her the upper hand in this conversation. She was taking power from Dr Setchell, as if something else could be more important than those incriminating photos.

"I'm finalizing a paper for the government. It would be good to get your initial response."

"I can't imagine how I could be of help with your work? What is it about?"

"I'm sure there will be representatives from West Beach invited to the forthcoming summit on population."

"I don't know anything about it Dr Silwood."

"No? It would be something the science and medical teams will be involved in."

"They don't come under my management as I'm sure you are aware. I liaise with them but my responsibilities are the fabric of the building and security. As far as they are concerned I'm just facilities management."

"Yes. I understand the structure. Obviously the care of the men falls under your overview and for that reason I know it is something you have an interest in. I hoped you wouldn't mind indulging me with a little of your time so that I can tentatively run some ideas past you."

"Try me. What is on your mind?"

"I still have to finalize the report and discuss it with my colleagues, but I am thinking that if the government wants to crack the fertility problem, stabilize and increase the population, we need to be looking for more births each year."

"And you have some proposals for achieving this?"

"Actually, no. I don't know how it can be done. However, I can see that there is an unnecessary focus on the low male birth rate. We have fixated on this fact rather than looking at the real problem. The problem isn't enough total births, but not enough girls. We should be focusing on encouraging fertile women to have more children and increasing the number of fertile women of childbearing age. Even without medical intervention, if the women who can have children have more, then within twenty to thirty years we will see a considerable growth in the birth rate. Many more women, a few more men and statistically some of those extra babies will grow up to be fertile themselves thereby adding to the pool of potential parents."

"You don't propose any intervention to increase

the male population?"

"It isn't necessary for the rise in population so it is irrelevant to the subject of this summit."

"That's very interesting."

"To be honest I haven't rehearsed this pitch or tested it on my colleagues and I'm wondering if it falls anywhere?"

"What you're saying makes perfect sense to me." Setchell nodded, fully appreciating the implication. No increase in the male birthrate meant security for her position and West Beach for decades into the future.

"Of course, it is good for your business here. It would increase the work of the medics involved in fertility." Mia didn't need to spell out the full mutual benefits of the proposal.

"Yes, I can see that. It will also be politically acceptable if increasing males isn't on the agenda. What I didn't get is how your team, at Exlabs, could benefit?"

"That may be my biggest problem. I need my boss behind me."

"Your pitch, as you call it, could result in perhaps financial incentives for women to have more children and with no extra funding to science at all. The doctors here would be happy with the extra work. We benefit and personally, I am delighted with maintaining the way things are but I can't see the owners of Exlabs being happy with your proposal. As you have outlined it to me, there is nothing in it for them."

"If there is extra funding available it might be for fertility drugs for women, this is an area we could bid for funding in."

"I know our scientists are working in that field

right now, they would automatically jump the queue for additional funding in their field."

"Yes I know that too. So the difficulty I will have is winning the support of my CEO to back this proposal."

"West Beach scientists are the only players in that game and the scientists with the strongest case will be those who collaborate with our team."

"Your team will benefit if other scientists are arguing the same case alongside them, not putting up counter proposals against them. We will be up against strong and popular arguments for alternative technologies supported by women that want to wipe West Beach off the map."

"A mutual collaboration would be in both of our interests. I wonder, Dr Silwood," Dr Setchell paused for thought. "When do you have to put your paper to your colleagues?"

"Tomorrow, at the very latest, today would be ideal."

"You should meet with our science director first and discuss a collaboration. Do you have time I will find out if she can see you straight away?"

"Yes, that would be excellent. I have met her before but not discussed these ideas."

&&&

"It is all over for us unless we take drastic measures.

Statisticians claim that the population is decreasing and, if left to nature, our species is facing extinction. This is the conclusion of a new report entitled Women Only, which advocates the use of various techniques of artificial reproduction using only female cells.

The report comes just ahead of a government summit to look at the population and reproduction crisis. The timing must be no coincidence. Popular opinion supports methods that will give us more girls and no boys but they are controversial..."

Extract from a contemporary news item. Published that day.

Chapter Fifteen

Check

Rayfe was sitting in the outside rest and recreational area concentrating on a game of afternoon chess when he became aware of a figure beside him. He looked up to see the familiar face of Walsh, she didn't look at him she was studying the board as intently as he had been. This was no time to be distracted; checkmate was within a few moves so long as his opponent didn't spot it.

Rayfe made his move. It was poker face time so he prayed Walsh wouldn't give it away. His opponent gave Walsh only a cursory glance and moved a pawn. Cody wasn't in Walsh's group so if she were here for any reason other than to watch chess it would involve Rayfe and not Cody.

"Checkmate, my friend."

"Oh, no," Cody put his hand to his head seeing the trap that had been set, just when it was too late.

"Did you want me?" Rayfe looked up to Walsh;

otherwise he'd be setting the pieces up for a rematch.

"I would like to pull you away, yes."

The men said their goodbyes and Rayfe stood up.

"Let's go for walk Rayfe, enjoy the end of summer while we still can." Walsh was dressed entirely in black, as always. Black trousers, belt, top and boots, predictable. It marked her out from the guards, no mistaking, she wasn't one of them.

They walked towards the sports courts where teams of men were practicing their ball control. Autumn was approaching, the afternoon sun wasn't so hot and the sea breeze made it perfect for afternoon exercise.

"I haven't seen you since you moved into your new room, how is it?"

"It's good. At first it felt like we had so much space to spread out but we've got used to it now."

"So now you'd like to share with just one person, not three?"

"I don't know about that. It would be good, but I do like the guys, we get on well. Zander said it was your idea that we work as a team, and that has been positive. Of course, we've got spare beds so we could get new men joining us."

"I may not meet up with you very often Rayfe, but I have known you, Zander and the others since you each arrived here at the age of nineteen. Not only do I think you four are each capable of being among the most popular men here, for our customers, I also was sure you would get on well. Yes, I thought your personalities would gel as a team. Not everyone can you know. I think the age gap between you helps as well. Each of you brings skills to share, even the youngest men in your team have things that you can all learn from."

"To be honest I couldn't see that at first. I thought it was the kids, as Zander calls them, learning from us but over the five months I've gained from them so I know exactly what you are saying."

"They are both mature for their ages, both quite unique individuals, I think they will surprise you. I will be keeping a very close eye on you four over the coming months."

They walked some more.

"If we do agree to put another man in your room we will have to be careful not to upset the balance there." Walsh seemed to be talking to herself, thinking aloud. Perhaps she had someone in mind.

"One of West Beach's most important clients is very keen on you Rayfe. I'm sure you know that."

Taken aback, Rayfe instantly pictured Mia, who was never far from his thoughts. She was keen on him but had said that she wouldn't be seeing him again so it couldn't be her. In addition, Walsh said one of the most important clients, he didn't know how women would achieve that status but he thought it meant women who had been visiting for decades, older women, so it couldn't be Mia. Although she did get invited to the picnic. Perhaps his admirer was one of the women from the picnic?

"Who do you mean?" the confusion on his face wasn't an act, he genuinely didn't know.

"Mia, of course, who else?"

"How does she qualify as a most important client?"

"You don't know?" Walsh looked surprised, this was going to be a drawn out conversation. "Well I shouldn't say that, perhaps, because they are all important and should be treated as such but Mia is very important. A V.I.P. because of her influential role in the science community. She could be a powerful ally and advocate for our work here."

"Our work? I don't really understand."

"Hasn't she told you about her work?"

"A bit, not really. Look, I don't know what you're talking about." She had told him and he had listened but her science research made no connection with his life at WB.

"I'm talking about the science side of WB. As long as births require men, plenty of men, you are all safe here. Life at West Beach can continue as normal. Mia has a lot of influence and can argue that case well. Others are arguing for a future without West Beach, and that could seriously jeopardize the future for you men here and all men everywhere."

"I see. She said she was a scientist, but I never realized the connection. I didn't know she was so important." It dawned on Rayfe that although he had heard Mia talking about her work he hadn't really listened. He knew the subject, of course, but didn't comprehend the pivotal role of Mia's input, that it was her work that could shape the future. If he'd really listened carefully he might have understood why she couldn't devote herself to him right now.

"Important is an understatement! She is very modest. You wouldn't guess what a powerful and clever woman she is just from looking at her."

"You've met her?" This surprised him.

"Yes. She's lovely isn't she."

"Yes. But why are you telling me about this?" ask Rayfe.

"She's in love with you isn't she? So I thought you might like to know more about her and how it is crucial that she remains a friend of WB."

Rayfe didn't know what to do with the information, but he didn't want to share with Walsh the details of his last encounter with Mia. It still hurt. Walsh may be right about Mia being influential, but she was wrong about her being in love with him. He felt abandoned like a used toy, discarded, as clients used all of the men here, used them over and over. The encounters were okay, he thought, so long as feelings weren't involved because that is how people got hurt. He found out the hard way.

He still couldn't believe what Mia had said to him. Her reasons for not seeing him made no sense to him unless she was maliciously messing with his head and his heart. Perhaps what Walsh was saying about Mia as a VIP was relevant. He hadn't thought of her in this way, and perhaps if he had understood that she was considering a bigger picture than just the two of them, things may have been different.

"I'm still not sure why you are telling me this, as in how is this going to affect the way I relate to her?"

"She like's you how you are, so certainly don't change. However, it is worth knowing that things could be different in contrast to most clients. For example, she may visit more frequently, she could be your guest with no fees to pay, and we might invite her to access more areas of the unit. Perhaps she might stay overnight. I don't know exactly what she'd like to do but whatever she wants we will make it happen for her."

"Special treatment."

"Yes, in a way, but it isn't unique. There are other women who also get special treatment. I should say other couples. If she stays overnight it won't be so she can stay on her own, will it?"

"Well, thanks for the tip off. Is there anything else I should know? You said you met her, did she say anything about me?"

"She is very focused on her work. My tip for you might be to take an interest in it because it is important to her. You know in general people like you to be interested in what they are interested in but I don't need to tell you that."

"No, you don't need to remind me. You taught me that when I arrived here, and I have been using it as a winning technique ever since," he smiled as he spoke. Walsh had been more than a good trainer, in his early years he thought of her as a good friend.

"And did she say anything about me?" He persisted with the question that he'd already asked.

"We talked about you. I can't repeat what she said but she also comes here for her work and she's very professional."

Rayfe wasn't sure what to do with the information. If Walsh was just here to tell him Mia is a VIP client, she might as well just tell it to whomever Mia booked in the future, as Rayfe felt sure it wouldn't be him.

"You could call her. Don't forget that. You could use what you've got to make her take notice of you Rayfe. A strong independent professional like her would be a bit intimidating for most of the men here but I know you can rise to the challenge. I guess I want you to know that I'm here if you need to make something happen. If you want to invite her to visit and stay with you, I can help set it up. You don't have to be just available when she books. You can do the chasing yourself if you really like her. I am right aren't I? You do like her that much?"

"Yes," *I love her.*

"Then let her know, Rayfe. You could call her, chase her. Invite her as your guest. She loves you too. Make her know WB isn't just about sex for money. We can make arrangements for couples in love."

"What sort of arrangements?"

"What do you want, to live together? Because I must admit anything is possible but that would be difficult. To stay together several nights a week is perfectly possible. To go out off site and even to go away for a few days is possible. There are places you can go together."

"What kind of places?"

"We have arrangements with various off-site venues. There are hotels and the like that do accept men into them. You know, some of your clients run businesses like that and being broad-minded women themselves they are willing to make their services available to couples like you and Mia. Of course, there aren't that many couples like you and Mia. Serious attachment between men and women is uncommon. Many women just like to see men here for fun without getting involved in complicated relationships, but something tells me you and Mia are the complex romantic relationship type."

"I need to think about it, to be honest. I'm not sure how I feel or what I want."

"Talk to Mia about all this."

"Can I get in touch with you in the next few days?" he asked. The men could always get in touch with Walsh so the statement was more to indicate that he would be getting in touch soon about this very issue,

"Great. Don't leave it too long to let her know she's special and you want to show her how special she is to you."

DEVIANT

&&&

"The Mother Superior of The New Matriarchal Church supports the proposals for Women Only reproduction. This surprise announcement comes in the wake of the report published yesterday warning that relying on men was doomed to catastrophe.

Previously, the religious order have refused to comment on issues of science and reproduction but in an interview the Mother Superior made her reasons clear. The church disapprove of sex outside a long term committed relationship and, therefore, are fundamentally opposed to the funding of the West Beach fertility services through the running of a Brothel at the same location.

When pressed on the subject of sexuality the Mother Superior said she prayed for those sinners who sought casual relationships. She urged such women to help themselves by seeking the available treatment.

"No woman should desire union with a man in this age," she said."

Extract from a contemporary news item.

Chapter Sixteen

Missing You

As ever Mia threw herself into her work, which wasn't difficult as there was always more to do than one woman could realistically achieve.

She liked to be very busy. Mia had met with Professor Johnston who was pleased with the draft paper and was positively delighted with the possibility of a partnership with West Beach on fertility research. The close working relationship forged by Mia between the two organizations within just a few weeks that made such a partnership approach possible, impressed Johnston. In this respect, Mia had pulled off a coup that stood Exlabs in good stead for future funding. That was tantamount to the highest seal of approval and a guaranteed job for life (if only guarantees of jobs for life were possible).

Still Walsh played in Mia's mind. Just she had loitered about the corridors, Walsh was now hovering in her head to keep thoughts of Rayfe right there.

When she had told him that was the end of her

visits to men, it seemed to make perfect sense. Well, it did before the words came out of her mouth. In her head it made sense. She could see the relationship was going nowhere, barely a relationship and how could it be when they were like prisoners in separate camps. Meeting Rayfe threatened all that she had worked so hard to achieve in her career. When the words poured out of her, becoming real, they sounded so different. Mia was taken aback by the way he reacted. He was genuinely upset and she did know why she hadn't expected that when recently he had said he loved her. His feelings for her were obvious but having a relationship was unfamiliar territory and not simple to navigate.

A few days on and Mia wished she'd never uttered those words, what was she thinking? She wanted to see Rayfe again, fall into his arms like nothing bad had happened, as if the painful conversation hadn't taken place. She wanted to see him, hold him and, yes, fuck him.

She could see him, she just had to book the appointment in the usual way and hope he didn't refuse to see her. Even if he did see her, they were going to have to address that conversation, and she just didn't know how she could sweep it away. She felt such a fool, surely, her behavior had ruined any genuine feelings he had for her. One day he proclaims his love for her and the next she tells him she's not going to see him again, like as if he isn't that important to her. She told him she loved him too but in the same breath she forcefully told him that he wasn't important enough for her to make the effort to see him again.

What was she thinking? Was she having some kind of mental melt down? If so, she only deluded herself for a moment.

Rayfe was the most important thing in her life of that she was certain. More important than her work. More than the population crisis, which she hadn't given much thought to up until a few months ago. And he was a lot more interesting than bio-fuel.

She had what she wanted, the real man and his real feelings, but she had sabotaged her own dream-come-true moment. How she regretted it and wished she could turn the clock back and take back those words.

Then there was Joanne Walsh rubbing salt in the wounds, reminding her how lucky she was to win his heart. If only there was something she could do.

Rayfe phoned and invited her to West Beach, she was astonished. Delighted to have a second chance and she knew she'd have to find the words to repair the damage. The call was brief, neither Rayfe nor Mia mentioned their last encounter. He invited her to visit him as soon as possible.

***

Mia slipped through the familiar doors at the reception of West Beach to find Rayfe waiting for her. Wearing blue jeans and a T-shirt, every time she saw him he looked more irresistible in the flesh than she recalled in her mind and yet in her mind he was irresistible.

"I know we need to talk, but I am taking the very fact that you agreed to come and meet me as a good sign."

"In what way good?" Mia asked.

"A good sign that you might want to see more of me."

"I do want to see more of you," the words slipped from her mouth before she had time to control them, without intentionally creating the double meaning that was so familiar in their dialogue. The ice was broken, and they both smiled.

She moved closer to touch him, but he had already opened a door from the inner lobby of the reception into the private area of West Beach, not the usual door that led to the rooms.

"This way." Rayfe led her into the corridor with the windows that looked out over the pool and acres of grounds, he stopped at the first door and, taking her hand firmly in his, he led her through.

"This is our side of the wall," Rayfe announced. "Welcome to WB."

It happened so quickly, gut instincts kicked in and fear seized Mia, based on a lifetime of prejudice, she was scared. Outnumbered in the men's world where they might not be as kind to her as when she met them on a one to one basis; the fears of her sister came to mind. She hadn't realized he'd be bringing her here, on the phone they hadn't discussed what they were going to do.

"The music arena, the pool, the rest and recreation area," Rayfe announced, pointing out the obvious features of the immediate area. Oblivious to her nervousness, he welcoming her with a tour as if it was the most natural thing in the world. There were a few men in the pool swimming lengths. The recreation area next to the pool looked like an outside version of Stella's bar. There was a small bar, presumably just for drinks, no food. Tables and chairs set out perhaps ten tables with four chairs each but more table and chairs stacked in a corner covered by a sturdy all-weather gazebo.

They had stepped into a crowded noisy space. Men were sitting chatting, drinking and playing cards. Three men were performing on a small stage, two guitarists and a drummer. All were engrossed in what they were doing and largely ignored her. A few glanced at her, there were even some friendly smiles but most didn't even see her.

"It's fairly sheltered from the wind in the R and R area so it is used most of the year it's just in awful weather or rain that we move inside."

"You play guitar here?" her voice sounded calm, though she didn't feel it. She moved closer to him, almost clinging on to him for safety.

"Yes. There's music performed or practiced out here most afternoons and evenings so we sign up to a rota."

"Do most men play something?" she asked.

"Most probably do, but the ability level is very varied."

"Come this way." They walked away from the pool area and Mia struggle to take in all that she was seeing because of the conflicting emotions inside. The anxiety due to being suddenly there and the turmoil about the discussion they needed to have.

"Is it okay for me to be here?" she whispered.

"Yes, of course it is." He looked at her, and she looked back, deep into his eyes seeking reassurance.

"I live here, and you are my guest, it's fine. I thought you might like to see where I live."

"I seem to remember you inviting me to live with you before," Mia teased.

"And that offer still stands." Rayfe sounded

remarkably earnest given the ridiculousness of the proposal. "I'm taking you to see my room and I can take you anywhere, just say what you'd like to see."

It was with wide eyes and trepidation that Mia walked through the grounds, she stared at the men with a combination of fear and curiosity. They in turn were friendly, they acknowledged her but didn't pay too much attention. If the situation was reversed and Rayfe was walking the streets in the capital, Mia shuddered to imagine, they could both be lynched.

Rayfe stopped at a door, E12. He knocked then opened the door and looked in. She stayed behind waiting for an invited to enter.

"Come in and meet one of my roommates." Rayfe held the door wide open and a giant figure moved somewhere inside. "Mia this is Zander, I call him Zee."

Mia liked the way Rayfe was so big, she associated it with his masculinity, but Zander was slightly taller and Mia thought he looked terrifying. He had long hair and his sleeveless shirt revealed heavily tattooed arms.

"Mia, Rayfe's talked about you, a lot," said Zander.

Mia felt herself blush, was this the most embarrassing thing ever? What could Rayfe be saying about her? Talking about their sexual encounters or about the times she had done things she'd like to forget? And she could remember a time that Rayfe had spoken about his roommates, or could she?

"It's good to meet you," Mia said. "I met another man before, Paul?"

"Paul and Jay are the other two in here," Rayfe explained. "Except they're not in here now."

"They're working, they'll be sorry they missed you," Zander added.

"I hope we didn't wake you." Now she was in the spartan room she could see that Zander must have jumped down from a top bunk bed when they arrived.

"No, not at all. OK, I was having a little quiet time but I need to get going to band practice so don't worry. You didn't disturb me."

"I wasn't worried!" replied Rayfe.

"I knew you wouldn't be." Zander gave Rayfe a friendly gentle punch to the shoulder and sauntered towards the door.

"Please excuse me for now, I'm sure we'll meet again."

"Yes, I hope so," Mia said, just to be polite. Rayfe's roommate he may be, but she couldn't imagine wanting to see him again anytime soon.

Zander left them alone and Rayfe finally released Mia's hand.

"He's being tactful, of course." Rayfe said, pulling at a chair for her to sit on. "Look, I'm sorry about how things went on the beach. I didn't think about how difficult things might be for you. I invited you here because I hope we can have another chance?"

"I'm so sorry Rayfe. You don't have to be sorry for anything. I acted like such a fool, and I've regretted it ever since. I didn't mean what I said, I don't know why said those things. I've always wanted to see more of you."

"Well, I need to make sure you know one thing."

"What?"

"When I said you could live with me I didn't mean in here." He looked around throwing his arms wide apart. "Not in this room, even though we've two spare beds."

She laughed, "I didn't think you were serious."

"I am serious about you. I love you and I don't want to be without you. We just need to work out how to make things work for us." He took her hands in his and looked sincerely into her eyes.

"I need to explain. I don't know how exactly, but let me try. I've found it difficult leading this secret double life. My work's stressful. A big part of me wants to change the world and another part of me wants to just hide."

Rayfe leaned towards her, listening intently.

"Everyone I talk to seems to think things are good the way they are, and I can understand what you are saying about life being good for you men in here. It just doesn't seem right to me but I am coming around to your way of thinking, I just need time. I'm twenty-nine years old and two years ago I had never met a man, so I have been going through some significant life changing experiences."

"I've had a life changing experience too. The world isn't perfect, Mia. That's obvious. But I only grasped

"So what next?"

"I have a few ideas. And before you think the wrong thing none of my ideas involve undressing you in this room where someone could walk in at any minute!"

"Shame," she teased.

"I want to see more of you. I wouldn't expect you to want to live here, but you might want to visit more often, to stay the night, perhaps, sometimes as my guest. I've talked with the powers that be and you won't have to pay to see me, ever. Though if you want to see someone else you will need to make some arrangement."

"I don't want anyone else," Mia protested.

"Good." He leaned forward and kissed her. At long last. A tender and loving kiss.

&&&

"Scientific adviser, Kerry Roth, refuted the claims made by Daughters of Scum that the last woman to live is currently alive.

There is no crisis. This is the official message from the government who have confirmed a secret summit on population growth is to be convened within the coming week."

Extract from a contemporary news item. Published that day.

Chapter Seventeen

Keeping the Secret

Mia felt she was floating out of West Beach, only two hours after arriving, with a great burden lifted from her. The guided tour, the much-needed talk with Rayfe and the incredible plan for the weekend all gave her so many positive things on which to feast her thoughts. The past few hours, days and weeks had been an emotional roller coaster, but she had a glimpse of the potential for a new life, a new life that would start tomorrow.

With her head in the clouds, wondering what to pack for the weekend she walked straight into another woman in the lobby with such force that they both almost fell over. The woman, who was also facing towards the door so was obviously also leaving the building, had stopped suddenly to look inside a briefcase.

"Sorry," said Mia and the woman turned to look at her.

"'Minetta! What are you doing here?" Mia was stunned to see her boss, surprise equally registering on the Professor's face.

"Professor Johnston! I didn't know you were going to be here."

"I came to see Professor Parker as we, hopefully, will be working more closely, thanks to your excellent work; but I didn't see you in there."

Obviously not, Mia wasn't in the science wing so there weren't too many other places she could have come from.

"I wasn't in that part of the building."

"Oh." Johnston's eyes opened wide.

For a fleeting moment, Mia toyed with admitting the truth. It would be a relief not to hide but she was fairly certain it would be the end of her career. The end of her life as she knew it, and this wasn't the right time for career suicide.

"I've had a tour of the men's unit," She stuck to the truth, up to a point. "Dr Setchell, the facilities director here, arranged it for me." Thinking fast under pressure, Mia's brain was feeding her mouth the best possible answers to get her out of this tight spot.

"I see. Was it interesting?"

"Yes fascinating, have you ever seen inside?"

"No, I've never given it any thought."

"As I said, Dr Setchell suggested I would find it useful, background, you know. It was nothing like I might have imagined. Not that I have imagined it." Mia added trying not to appear flustered. In a moment of inspiration, she thought to cover herself in case of being caught out in a similar way in the future. "Apparently, there is more to see, and they insist I come again another time."

"That's very brave of you. Let's go to the station together and you can tell me about it and I'll tell you about my meeting. Are you getting the train home now or going back to the lab?"

The stream train service terminated at West Beach but also served the science park on its route to The Capital. Mia couldn't think of an excuse to go back to the lab, much as she didn't want to spend the journey home on the train with her boss. She wanted to daydream about the past two hours with Rayfe, rerun their conversations, think about what she had seen and perhaps list the things she needed to pack for her weekend away. Johnston, however, wanted to talk about their new alliance with the West Beach science team, developing new fertility drugs. She was sure new funding would be coming their way after the imminent summit.

"Doing things like what you have just done, is beyond your normal duties. It's not chemistry, it's not biology, it is outside of our remit."

Mia listened in silence, speaking could land her in trouble.

"And it is brilliant. It shows real dedication to the issue. It's all thanks to you. I see a very bright future for Exlabs. Looking at things in a fresh way, considering solutions that wouldn't occur to other scientists who are dogmatic in their thinking. That is why I wanted you to lead this investigation. Thank you, Mia, it won't be forgotten."

Mia wondered if the sentiment would be the same if Johnston knew the truth about her. She doubted it.

***

"Zander, can you keep a close eye on the kids tomorrow? You boys will have to cope without me for a couple of days," said Rayfe.

The full dream team from E12, Zander, Jay, Paul and Rayfe had gathered beside the pool, as most of the men did in the evenings if they weren't with a client. A trio was playing some mellow reggae instrumental music. It was busy but as it was early, most men weren't settling here for the evening but passing through before going to dinner or to see a client. As all the roommates were available at the same time, Rayfe rounded them up for a conference to share his news.

"Judging by that grin on your face you're booked for the whole weekend by your favorite lady," Zander replied.

"Is it that obvious?"

A chorus of, "Yes" from his friends, told him they read him like a book.

"So do we get to know her name?" asked Paul.

"Mia, you met her before, at the picnic."

"I remember her. I'm pleased you two made up, you seemed to have a bit of a falling out that day." Despite his youthfulness, Paul seemed sincere, as if he understood that Rayfe had genuine feelings for Mia.

"We've moved on since then. She was here earlier for a tour; I would have introduced you all." Rayfe was talking to the group, but looking at Jay, who was the only man who hadn't met her.

"She seemed nice, I hope I didn't seem rude

running off like that, but I thought you might want some privacy in our room." Zander was perched on the edge of his chair. Swaying with the music, his attention seemed divided between his roommates and the band.

"You had a woman in our room!" Jay sat forward, wide-eyed with amazement.

"We didn't do anything, I just showed her round."

"You were showing a lady backstage, here and we missed it?" Jay glanced at Paul.

"Yeah, where were you guys? Booked?" Rayfe asked.

"Yes, together. We had a threesome. With all this working together, we must be set to hit the leader board. We've been seeing a client a day for weeks."

"But are they the wealthy ones?" Zander asked, sitting back in the chair. "You need the wealthy clients. You're definitely on the right track though." Fingering his long hair and looking relaxed he continued, "Mia, is she the one you've been pining for?"

Rayfe didn't answer just struggled to control his grin.

"Of course she's the one, you can see it on his face," Paul answered for him.

"I thought so when I saw you with her earlier."

"Are you going to spend the weekend cooped up in those rooms?" It was Jay's turn to ask questions. "Or is she going to be coming to our room again? It is my turn to meet her, don't forget, I want to meet her."

"We'll see," Rayfe smiled, not sure that he wanted to share too much with his roommates.

"He wants to keep her to himself, isn't that

obvious?" Zander interjected. "One day you youngsters will find love, too, and then you'll understand why Rayfe wants to be locked away in a room with her."

"I wouldn't mind being locked away in a room with a woman who wants a lot of what I've got to give." Always enthusiastic and always ready with a comment. Jay continued, "I'd like to crawl out the next day without the energy left to walk, or better still, you guys come in and get me. Carry me out. But I can't see myself being in love."

"You've just not found the right woman yet, Jay. And then you'd know love isn't about the sex. It is about enjoying being with a special person and wanting to be with them," Zander explained and Rayfe nodded in agreement. Everyone was smiling except Paul, who was biting his lip and looking lost in thought.

"Paul," Rayfe prompted, his friend had started to look quite ill, the color had drained from his skin, and his eyes glazed with far away thoughts.

Paul leaned forwards and without smiling, eyes flitting between the three of them he said, "You can't control who you fall in love with but it's not all good. It hurts when you can't see that person, and you can't do anything about it." Paul stood up, with a small smile forced onto his lips he added, "That's right isn't it, Rayfe."

"Yes."

The three men watched in silence as Paul disappeared in the direction of the village.

"I had no idea he was love with someone," said Zander, "Do you know who it is, Jay? You spend the most time with him."

"No, he's never said anything like that to me,"

Jay replied. "Perhaps I've not given him the chance." Jay looked a little regretful.

For a moment Rayfe forgot his own elation, Paul was completely right, not being able to contact Mia, and having no control over their relationship had felt like a private torture. Perhaps that young man was going through the same. Rayfe had never felt like this before and Paul was ten years his junior, but perhaps younger men could also fall in love.

&&&

"Women should not be slaves to animal urges. A blessing of the post-pandemic epoch is that we are free of an out of control libido. If you are not, then help is available. Consultations are private, confidential and free. This vital service is funded via the Matriarchy."

Extract from an advert.

Chapter Eighteen

Hamlet

Rayfe's invitation, for a weekend away, couldn't have come at a better time. Two days off work and the first substantial downtime Mia had enjoyed in months. Johnston emphasized that Mia must not do any work, have a serious break so she would be refreshed for the summit, the papers had been submitted and circulated to all interested parties.

Mia packed a bag of everything. The coastal weather at this time of year was unpredictable, it could be hot or cold, stormy or an Indian summer. If she didn't have the correct clothes for the weather Mia was sure they could always find sanctuary in the bedroom but part of the appeal of a weekend away was to get to know Rayfe better, not just staying in one room as they do at WB. Whilst she was mostly excited, she was also just a little apprehensive. In what sort of place would they be staying? She had no idea that men could stay anywhere outside of one of the men's units, not safely anyway.

Rayfe was ready and waiting for her just inside the familiar West Beach doors. He looked as eager and excited as she felt. He gave her a gentle kiss on the cheek, took her bag and her hand with his other and led her along through the familiar private door the same private corridor that she had seen before. Today they proceeded past the windows to the very far end of the building and into the small room where they had gathered for the picnic.

The door to the private car park was already open and their driver and bodyguard for the weekend, one woman two roles, was waiting. She was standing next to an intimidating looking military vehicle. The high backed truck with massive all-terrain wheels had blacked-out windows. Primarily powered by electric batteries, but as a hybrid military vehicle, expensive bio-fuel was an alternative option. There was very little chance of outrunning a serious enemy in an electric car or on the treacherous tracks, tracks that were once roads but had no maintenance in seven decades. The heavily armored vehicle was discretely armed, designed for defense and the security of passengers in the unlikely event of encountering hostility.

The vehicle didn't follow the coast but drove inland a little way before turning in an easterly direction. They traveled in silence, Rayfe and Mia held hands but stared out the windows, trips into the wilderness were rare not just for Rayfe who hadn't left the vicinity of West Beach in ten years but also for Mia. She was one of the few women who left the capital daily for a commute, by train, to the science park on the south coast. Outside of the main populated centers and farmed rural areas the countryside was an abandoned wilderness, buildings had crumbled to ruins, roads disintegrated, eroded by weather and plant growth. Whole towns and cities were lost to new vegetation. Wild natural growth and embryonic new forests were in the making.

After almost an hour of traveling, at a slow and steady but sometimes halting pace, they pulled up outside a small cottage in what appeared to be a tiny hamlet by the sea on the eastern coast. They had possibly traveled just ten or twenty miles or so, further along the coast at a more remote and less well visited spot.

An elderly woman came out to greet them, the sound of the vehicle must have alerted her to their presence.

"Welcome, you must be Mia and Rayfe, I am Grace," she greeted them as if it were perfectly normal to see males traveling with females.

Rayfe got their bags out of the vehicle and the guard drove a little further along the street before parking next to a cottage.

"Come, I'll show you around."

They followed in silence, glancing at each other and exchanging excited smiles.

"The guard will be staying there if you need her. I don't think you will." She pointed along the street. "This is your cottage for the weekend and I am next door. If you want me for anything, just knock."

The door was open. Mia and the old woman stood aside to let Rayfe enter first with the bags. He had to duck down and put one bag in front and one behind him to pass through the diminutive door. The women followed and Mia noticed that, fortunately, in the room beyond, Rayfe could stand up straight but he could also easily touch the ceiling. The front door opened onto a single room, an open plan ground floor with a basic kitchen at the back, a large fireplace and an open staircase against one wall.

"You should find everything you need in here. If it gets too cold, you can make a fire."

A stack of chopped logs and kindling were next to the fireplace. Although it was still summer, technically, the nights were drawing in and the nights could be chilly, so could the days.

"For food you'll want to come to the shop, which is the cottage after mine. It doubles as a cafe and everything else. It is the center of the village so anything you need you can probably find there. Finally, we have a pub at the end of the street, the building nearest to the sea. You can eat there in the evening if you want to. Dinner's at seven."

"Are there any other guests staying here at the moment?" Mia asked.

"No, only you and your driver. Apart from that it's just us permanent villagers here."

"Do you get many guests from West Beach?"

"We get more than you might think," Grace smiled and turned to Rayfe. "You don't need to hide here, not unless we get invaded, and that isn't likely."

"Has it ever happened?"

"Not in seventy years."

"How would you know? You're not that age," Rayfe joked.

"No, but this little oasis has been providing refuge for men and couples for the whole time. I took it over thirty years ago. Before that, I'd been a visitor like you."

They had seen a few other cottages, but the woman volunteered no further information.

"You can use the beach or wander freely in the

woods around here. We are miles from the nearest town. In fact, West Beach is as close as anywhere else is to here and you saw how long that took. Now, you didn't come here to spend time with me, but you know where I am if you need me."

Grace departed. Left alone in a strange house with Rayfe for just a moment Mia felt like her old self, vulnerable and shy but he took control of the situation.

"Let's look around." He took her hand, as they were standing in the only ground floor room this only left upstairs to explore. Rayfe led the way up to a landing with two doors, both stood open, one into a bijou bathroom above the kitchen, the other into the only bedroom. A large bed almost filled the room, with fresh, clean white sheets and a mini-mountain of well-stuffed pillows it looked comfortable and inviting.

Rayfe's hand tightened his grip on hers and he placed his other arm around her.

"I've missed you," he whispered as he bought his face close to hers and touched his lips to her. Soon they were kissing passionately, mouths locked together, tongues, teeth and saliva mingled together. Bodies pushed up close. Mia could feel his erection against her stomach and her own need, aching for him. He pulled her on to the bed on top of him. Both still dressed, kissing they thrust against each other, rutted. It had been too long since they had touched each other in the way they needed to.

"I want you," Mia whispered when she finally pulled her mouth from Rayfe's.

"How do you want me?"

"I want you in me, fucking me," she felt like she was burning with an overwhelming animal need.

Sure that Rayfe wanted the same she quickly got off him and tore off her clothes without the teasing that had accompanied their early encounters.

Rayfe was just as eager his hands went to his belt he slipped off his trousers, as she took her clothes off. Before he had time to finish undressing, a naked Mia was pulling at him. She climbing on top of him, condom already in her hands, she slid it on to him as he wriggled out of his T-shirt. His cock standing to attention, she lowered herself onto it.

For a moment, Mia thought that he couldn't be as desperate as she was for this because he had sex every day, whereas, for her their times together weren't nearly often enough. She quickly pushed the thoughts of Rayfe with other women from her mind.

Breathlessly she slowly moved up and down on his cock. Up until it was almost out, then down, down, and down feeling the long thick dick filling her and until her clit pushed against his skin.

He had been looking at her and rocking his hips in time with her, but he shut his eyes as Mia felt her own muscles involuntarily clenching his cock and submitted to her need to come. She thrust on to him more urgently, lifting her head back and moaning loudly. She totally lost control, lost consciousness just for a moment, what was happening to here? Eventually she returned to the here and now, still moving but less urgently. Rayfe gripped her more tightly and thrust in a similar way, with urgency. He shared her ecstasy, and she collapsed against him.

After a few minutes, she rolled off to lay cradled in his arms.

"Are you hungry?" he asked.

"Yes." And her stomach started growling as if acting on command.

"Me too. Let me go see what I can sort out."

"No pipeto, remember, no pipeto here," she giggled. She slid under the blanket and curled up as he stood and slipped back into his clothes.

"Of that one thing, I can promise you." He chuckled.

***

Mia stayed laying in the bedroom feeling comfortable and relaxed in a way that she hadn't done for months. She could hear noises downstairs but was soon surprised to smell the delicious greasy aroma of frying food. She got up to investigate, pulling on a long dress for decency, with no underwear.

"I wasn't sure whether you'd want food in bed?" He looked at home working the food in the frying pan.

"That seems a bit decadent; it is still the middle of the day."

"Well, do you want to set the table? I've found cutlery here."

"I never imagined you as a cook," Mia said.

"I can probably do many things you never imagined," he smiled. Of course, he'd done plenty of cooking, along with all the other domestic chores through his life. "We don't have servants at West Beach you know."

"I don't have servant's either, but my eating arrangements are usually pretty basic."

"In what way?"

"I live off quick snacks or eat out; I don't eat anything that will require too much work in my kitchen. In fact, what I have can barely be called a kitchen."

"Don't you live in a big house?"

"No. I live in a couple of rooms, about as big as

this cottage but in a shared building. That's partly why you couldn't visit. The neighbors would be suspicious. I never have guests, and they would hear your deeper voice. Not to mention the other noises we might make." Conspiratorial, knowing smiles passed between them. The food was almost ready, and hunger kept them from abandoning the meal.

"I had to go to the shop to get the food and you will never guess what."

"What."

"The lady who runs it was there."

"And?"

"With her husband."

"Her husband?"

"And she invited us to the village pub tonight where there will be a few couples, men and women, eating and dancing she says, at seven o'clock."

"No. You are teasing."

"Honestly, I'm not teasing."

"Did you know about this place? Have you been anywhere like this before?"

"No I didn't know about this, and I've not left West Beach since I arrived there. When I was nineteen. Never"

"I've heard rumors, but I thought they were just stories. Did no one talk about this at West Beach?" she asked.

"I never needed to know, Mia, because I've never met anyone special before, and this is obviously for people who are special, in love."

***

Mia wanted to solve some of the big problems in the world. She had known Rayfe only a few months, but it was good to see there were more options for the future than she had ever imagined. A life for a couple really was possible and Mia might need to rethink her future.

&&&

"*Daughters of Scum have confirmed that they propose a permanent picket outside of West Beach. They expect support from across social, political and religious groups...*"

THE END

ALMOST…

Do you want to know more about this Matriarchal society?
- There is exclusive content in my email/newsletter.
- Plus further novels and short stories in the pipeline.
- Find out more about the world that exists under Matriarchy and life in different Men's Units in the next novel set in this world. **ARRIVAL**, due to be published in November 2015.
- And a third **THE MAN**, is planned for early 2016.

You can sign up for H.J. Perry's email/newsletter to be alerted when future stories set in this world appear.

Sign up directly through the wordpress blog

https://helenjperry.wordpress.com/

The email includes notifications about special offers .

It also includes exclusive stories and insights into HJ's speculative thinking, stuff you can't find anywhere else.

Like the extras on a special edition DVD that features the Director's cut, deleted scenes and interviews with the actors. In 2015 email extras will include more stories from inside West Beach. Sexy stories featuring the characters in this book. Including that four-some with Rose.

If you enjoyed this you may enjoy more by Helen J Perry. Her author page is here:

More short erotic fiction by Helen J Perry

- *The L Words in **i.Lover** anthology **2015***

- *Broadstairs Bloke Week in **Who Thrilled Cock Robin** anthology **2015***

- *Quick reads, 5 short stories in **Nothing Personal***

- *Quick reads, 5 more short stories in **Nothing Too Personal***

- ***Lingam and Yoni Massage Lessons***

- ***Close Encounter** coming soon (October 2015)* **Bisexual Oral Appreciation Society** an erotic romance series

- ***The Libidians of Lowel*** (SF erotica)

About

The libidians are a humanoid alien species. The females are highly prized due to their sexy looks, hour glass figure but most importantly of all their incredible libido. Libidian females have an almost insatiable appetite for sex with no inhibitions and few boundaries.

Libidians feature in the story the L Words and in a series of forthcoming SF stories by Helen J Perry, due late 2015.

Broadstairs Bloke Week by **Helen J Perry** in the anthology **Who Thrilled Cock Robin** is a sexy F/M/M threesome story set in Folk Week and inspired by a folk song.

Nothing Personal by **Helen J Perry** and **Nothing Too Personal** by are collections of very short stories deliberately written to be quick reads at bed time, perhaps for reading aloud with a partner. All the stories have the theme of women having NSA sex with strangers in a wide range of situations.

Excerpt from **The Boxes** erotic SF written by H J Perry & Adria Kane.

The Boxes were an instant success, one of those business ideas that arrived at the right time and place, at that point in history when women wanted to buy sexual services in the same way that they bought groceries. Not online, click and collect or home delivery, although those methods were increasingly popular. The concept of supermarket-style instant gratification at a budget price spoke to women everywhere.

"For less than the price of a good lunch you can simply lie back and enjoy."

Most women would happily skip lunch once or twice a week in order to have an orgasm in a box. This allowed them to have their physical desires met without the tiresome requirement of finding a willing partner at random through a process of matchmaking, dating and elimination.

Within a few years, many women had tried The Boxes. The uptake was as great as nylons in the 1940s, microwaves in the 1980s or mobile phones in the 2000s. Within two years more women had visited them than owned an e-reader.

Like masturbation, visiting The Boxes was not something one would normally chat to friends and colleagues about. The reality of cheap services for all meant that after the removal of clothing from the waist down, women lay in a box and waited for things to happen to them. The marketing did not warn the uninitiated that the first impression was like lying in a coffin awaiting burial and being prepared for a C-section, at the same time. No matter how well padded and comfortable, there is no getting away from the fact that it was still a box. In fact, the upholstery added to the coffin-like feel of the casket.

Imagination was key to success. It was best to focus on the fact that once reclined, one's naked and exposed lower half is presented like a luxury gift to the person behind the curtain. Lined wooden cases contain only the finest merchandise, after all.

To read on find the book FREE at any ebookstore.

Printed in Great Britain
by Amazon.co.uk, Ltd.,
Marston Gate.